Master vampire Krispin Stearling has led his coven for over one-hundred-fifty years. Ruling his people while running a successful hotel and bar — which affords the vampires a safe, discreet place to search for donors — creates a great deal of stress. Krispin finds refuge on his rooftop garden and meditates there often. Imagine his surprise when his beloved literally falls out of the sky, taking out a swatch of bushes with him. After Krispin drives away his beloved's attacker, he takes him to his suite and ensures he's well cared for. He learns his name is Washington, and he's a tracker for the nearby Aerasceatle clutch. The gargoyle who'd injured him is a rogue he's been tracking. While Wash admits to wanting to pursue his bond with Krispin, he has reservations. Wash's clutch recently gained a new chieftain, a new inner circle, and he's just coming to terms with the changes. Can Krispin convince Wash that switching his loyalty once more, to a vampire no less, will be well worth the upheaval it'll cause to both their lives?

A Gargoyle for his Own
Copyright © 2020 Charlie Richards
ISBN: 978-1-4874-2967-6
Cover art by Angela Waters

Published by eXtasy Books Inc or
Devine Destinies, an imprint of eXtasy Books Inc

Look for us online at:
www.eXtasybooks.com or www.devinedestinies.com

A Gargoyle for his Own
A Paranormal's Love: Book Thirty

By

Charlie Richards

DEDICATION

Life takes you to unexpected places. Love brings you home.
~Unknown

CHAPTER ONE

"Good grief. That's the third fight Ridger has had to break up this evening. It's like there's something in the whiskey this evening."

Krispin Stearling, master vampire of the Maven coven, turned his attention to where Basques Grouper indicated. Scowling, he watched Ridger Carruthers escort a belligerent, angry-looking man out of the hotel bar. A second man was standing with a group of friends with his arms wrapped around his waist and his shoulders hunched. Another man had his arm slung around the upset guy's shoulders, clearly trying to console him. Carmine, an enforcer in Krispin's coven, stood with them, talking to them, probably offering a drink on the house and an apology.

"Hmmm," Krispin muttered. "It is odd." Smirking at Basques, he quipped, "Perhaps there's a full moon and we missed it?"

Basques scoffed. "Yeah. I'm sure that's it."

Over one-hundred-fifty years before, Krispin had started his coven with his best friends, Ridger and Basques. Ridger was his second-in-command, while Basques was his head enforcer. They'd settled in Green Springs, Wyoming, which had been little more than a mining town at the time. The first hotel they'd opened had also acted as a bawdy house, giving them access to a constant blood supply and leaving customers with happy memories.

Their business had evolved over the decades as the town

and laws changed. When Green Springs had eventually transitioned to a mostly tourist town, they'd built the massive hotel — *Clearmont Hotel and Suites*. Along with the standard indoor and outdoor pool, recreation room, spa, and exercise areas, there was a large hotel bar and lounge, a restaurant, a small business area, and even a dance club. Those were all located on the sprawling main floor. The following eleven floors were the hotel rooms. The remaining ten levels comprised of the vampires' suites.

There was plenty of opportunities for the fifty-seven vampires under Krispin's care to find blood sources.

"Here comes Ridger," Krispin pointed out, seeing his second reenter the lounge. "Perhaps he can clue us in."

Ridger bee-lined it to the bar where Krispin and Basques were sitting on bar stools. After putting in an order for a whiskey, he heaved a sigh and settled on a seat at Krispin's opposite side. Then he smirked at him.

It wasn't until Ridger had his drink in hand and the bartender — Page, a vampire in their coven — had moved off that he muttered, "An ex-boyfriend who wasn't too pleased to see his ex on a date with another guy."

"Ah."

Krispin didn't really have anything else to say. He'd never had a boyfriend, or girlfriend for that matter. As a paranormal who lived for centuries, he was waiting on Fate to bring him his special someone — his beloved — the one destined to bond with him and share their long lives together.

Sipping his whiskey, Krispin turned his mental energy in another direction. "Our hotel is booked for Memorial Day weekend. A lot of people coming to hike and explore the old mining museums."

"That's good," Ridger replied. Then he cocked his head as he narrowed his eyes. "But it's like that every year. What is it?"

Krispin smiled. His friends knew him so well. "But this is the first year we've had a flier in the coven," he pointed out quietly, referring to the fact that Basques had recently bonded with a small gargoyle named Dloben. After a glance around to make certain no humans were near enough to overhear, Krispin asked, "Have we confirmed that the airspace around the hotel and the surrounding buildings have all the cameras pointed in other directions?"

Basques nodded quickly. "Absolutely. He doesn't go far when he wants to stretch his wings, but we sure appreciate you accommodating him." Grinning, Basques winked, his deep-blue eyes twinkling, "And the fact that you're willing to share your rooftop oasis with us . . . thanks."

Scoffing softly, Krispin smirked at his friends. "My rooftop oasis," he muttered, shaking his head. "You both are welcome to use it. You always have been."

"We know," Ridger replied with a smile and a shrug of his wide shoulders. "But we also know how much the rooftop garden means to you. It's your sanctuary."

Krispin nodded once. His friends spoke the truth. Leading a coven of over fifty vampires while managing a hotel with several internal businesses created plenty of stress, even with the help of his best friends. When they'd put in the twenty-two-story building decades before, Krispin had needed somewhere to get away and meditate. The roof had been the perfect place to set up a garden with trees, bushes, flowers, trellises, and a fountain with benches. There was even a small greenhouse with similar features on a smaller scale for when it was winter.

While Krispin's friends occasionally went there to decompress, it wasn't often. For the most part, Krispin and the gardener — the vampire, Chase — had been the only regular visitors for years. With Basques bonding with Dloben, that had changed a little, but Krispin didn't mind.

"How is Dloben settling in?" Krispin asked.

Smiling happily, Basques answered, "Great. He's really blossoming." Then he rubbed his big hand over his thigh as he let out a sigh. "Still ends up a little jumpy around crowds." Basques waved his hand, indicating the busy lounge. "When it begins to clear out, he'll join me, but this is too much for him."

"So that's a no-go on the dance club then, huh?" Ridger pointed out.

"Oh, hell no," Basques replied, shaking his head. "Occasionally, we'll hit it for the first thirty minutes on a weeknight." Then his cheeks actually darkened as his mind went somewhere else. A second later, Basques told them, "And thirty minutes is more than enough to get my motor running." He laughed as he blinked and refocused on them. "Dloben has some damn fine moves."

Krispin chuckled softly as Ridger barked a laugh.

Basques nudged Krispin's arm with his elbow. "And he really does appreciate the access to your garden."

When Krispin had heard that Dloben had mostly worked in the kitchens of his gargoyle clutch, he'd figured as much. His old home had been an abusive place for a small gargoyle such as him—not that Krispin had known, at the time. Then one of the clutch's enforcers had managed to wrestle control and become the chieftain.

Chieftain Kinsey had changed many things in the clutch. Small gargoyles were no longer treated as second-class citizens. Dloben had begun working in their gardens, loving being outside.

Krispin figured he would enjoy the same at the coven.

"You know he's working with Chase now," Basques commented, returning Krispin's focus to their conversation. "I think our gardener appreciates the company."

"I'm glad to hear it." Krispin had *already* heard that, but it was good to hear confirmation from his friend. "He could use the help. The garden ended up a little larger than I'd anticipated."

Chuckling, Basques nodded.

"Speaking of which," Krispin commented before knocking back the rest of his whiskey. "It's getting late. I'm going to head up. I'll have my phone on me if anything arises that needs my attention."

Basques nodded. He was on management duty that evening. They rotated it between the three of them, so no one ended up burned out.

"Have a good one, Kris," Ridger offered before sweeping his gaze over the lounge. "I don't see what I'm after in here, so I think I'll head to the dance club." He waggled his brows and licked his lips.

Chuckling, Basques patted Ridger on his shoulder. "Happy hunting, my friend."

Krispin paused, watching Ridger head out of the room. He knew what his buddy planned to do. His vampire second was looking for a little action so he could feed.

Turning back to Basques, Krispin asked, "I bet you don't miss that, do you?"

Basques shook his head, a warm smile creasing the features as a faraway light entered his eyes. "Definitely not."

A pang of jealousy churned in Krispin's gut, and he quickly squashed it. He didn't want Dloben, but he did want what his head enforcer had found. At over two hundred years old, he was getting a little tired of waiting.

And, yet, continue to wait, I shall.

Krispin headed out of the lounge and crossed to the bay of elevators. Once inside the carriage he inserted a keycard into the slot and hit the button for the thirteenth floor. He and his inner circle lived on the floor directly above the last of the hotel rooms, which were on the twelfth level. They were the first line of defense and secrecy.

The vampire coven's floors could only be accessed with a keycard.

Once Krispin reached his suite, he headed straight for the bedroom, unbuttoning his suit jacket on the way. He tossed his wallet, keys, card, and phone on the nightstand. After that, he quickly stripped, placing his dirty clothes into the hamper.

Krispin took a short, hot shower, happy to wash off the stress of the day. After drying, he grabbed a pair of pale green lounging pants. He picked up his phone and keycard, slid his feet into a pair of house shoes, then left his suite.

The private elevator Krispin headed to could only be accessed by a select few, since it was the only one that reached the roof. Stepping inside, Krispin felt the anticipation filling him. He inserted his keycard before tapping the button for the roof.

As soon as the door swished open, revealing the warm evening, Krispin inhaled deeply. The fragrance of flowers, earth, and bushes filled his senses. The trickle of the fountain reached his ears. Soft lights illuminated the maze of the garden paths as well as the colorful plants.

Krispin smiled.

Stepping off the elevator, Krispin headed down a path to his right. His friend's assessment—rooftop oasis—really was accurate. He loved it up there.

Pausing at a storage closet set up against the wall of the greenhouse, Krispin pulled out his yoga mat. His penchant for yoga and meditation wasn't common knowledge in his coven. He liked to keep that little personal nugget to himself and a few trusted people—namely, Ridger, Basques, and now Dloben.

It wasn't that he was embarrassed by his nightly ritual. Instead, he just didn't care for the teasing he knew it would invite. What he got up to in private was his own business.

Placing the yoga mat on a grassy stretch near the fountain, Krispin stepped onto it and began his nightly routine. As he moved through different poses, focusing on his breathing and headspace, he felt the troubles of the day slip away. His mind cleared, and the muscles of his body warmed.

Perfect.

Krispin was just wrapping up his routine when an odd whooshing sound reached his sensitive ears. Cocking his head, he straightened and rested his hands on his hips. He narrowed his eyes and waited to see if it came again.

It did, accompanied by the unmistakable sound of flesh hitting flesh and a roar.

"What the hell?" Krispin peered around, searching for the source. "Who's fighting at my coven?"

To Krispin's shock, a movement to his right drew his attention just in time to watch a large form slam into a trellis, wiping it out. The body continued to tumble, carving a trail of dirt and destruction. A blueberry bush went next, followed by a bed of daylilies. Finally, the brown-skinned form came to a stop beside a pecan tree.

Krispin started toward it warily. He spotted black wings and realized he was staring at a gargoyle.

What the hell?

He was within twenty feet of the male when another gargoyle landed next to the fallen one. Instead of helping, the gray-hided gargoyle swung a black-clawed hand and flayed the skin of the brown gargoyle's back. Blood sprayed from the wound . . . hitting Krispin in the face and torso.

Licking his lips at it on reflex, Krispin discovered two things at once.

My beloved just fell from the sky right in front of me, and some motherfucker is trying to kill him.

Hell no!

Screaming a battle cry, Krispin lunged. With his vampire speed, he easily reached the attacker between one heartbeat and the next. He sliced his claws through one black wing as he sank the claws of the other into the gargoyle's back, right about where the kidney should be.

The gargoyle bellowed and leaped forward, jumping away from Krispin. He pivoted and spread his thick arms and wide wings.

"Stay out of this, vampire," the male ordered.

"You landed on the roof of my coven house," Krispin stated. "No unsanctioned attacks will take place here. State your name and business."

No way was he going to tell the bastard of his discovery. He didn't know what was going on between the two males, but he wasn't going to allow him to hurt his beloved.

Sneering, the gargoyle stated, "As if you could stop me."

The male lunged forward, but Krispin was ready. He pivoted and swung, slicing his three-inch talons into the gargoyle's side. The male was clumsy, thinking his massive, six-foot-six frame gave him an advantage.

Krispin hadn't kept hold of his coven for one-hundred-fifty years with words alone. He'd been in his fair share of fights. He easily evaded the gargoyle's attempts to hit him, countering with blows to the creature's torso, thighs, and wings each time.

After Krispin's third slash to the gargoyle's wings, the other paranormal bellowed with rage as he lifted off the ground. At first, Krispin thought he would dive-bomb him or something. Instead, he flew away, yelling that it wasn't over.

Krispin watched the gargoyle until he was out of sight in the dark sky.

"Moron doesn't even know if he's being watched by a human," Krispin grumbled, shaking his head. "What the fuck?"

Then a low moan caught his attention, returning his focus to his downed beloved.

Rushing to the male's side, Krispin took in the flayed hide

of his back and one wing. He grimaced as he knelt beside him. As much as he wished he could begin licking the wounds to seal them, he didn't know the male or what had brought him here.

But I will soon.

The fact that he hadn't woken yet was cause for concern, too.

"Right, get my head out of my ass."

Krispin jumped to his feet and rushed back to his yoga mat. He grabbed his phone and dialed Basques's number. His enforcer picked up on the second ring just as Krispin dropped back to his knees beside the gargoyle.

"Hey, buddy," Basques greeted. "All's quiet here. No need to—"

"Shut up a sec," Krispin cut him off. "I need you to locate Ward and bring him and Dloben up to the roof. Ridger, too, if he's not with a donor."

"I'm on the move," Basques replied instantly, and the noise of the lounge disappeared from the background. "I'll bring everyone up as quickly as I can. What's going on?"

Unable not to touch, Krispin threaded his fingers through the gargoyle's shaggy, dark-brown hair, pushing it away from his face. "My mate just fell from the sky. Literally."

"What the fuck?"

Krispin felt about the same. "He's a gargoyle. He was attacked, and he's injured. Unconscious. I was wondering if Dloben would recognize him."

"Damn, Kris," Basques muttered through the line. "Congrats, and don't worry. I'm sure he'll be fine." Then a laugh erupted from him.

"What?" Krispin didn't know what his buddy could find funny about the situation.

"Guess you're stuck carryin' your offspring, just like me."

Krispin felt his gut twist and his ass clench. Gargoyles could get their male mates pregnant.

"Oh, fuck."

CHAPTER TWO

"Do you recognize him?"

The tenor voice pierced Washington's pain-addled mind, deep, melodious, and soothing, urging him toward consciousness.

So tired. Why am I so tired? Why am I in pain?

Washington—Wash to his buddies—couldn't answer either of those questions.

"Yeah. That's Washington. He's a tracker for the clutch."

That voice Wash recognized.

Dloben.

But why am I hearing him?

Wash knew the small, pale-blue gargoyle had mated with a vampire. A man named Basques.

Wait . . . Basques . . . Dloben.

As Wash's recent memories slammed into him, he let out a low groan. He shifted his arm restlessly, trying to get it under him so he could push up. When he spread his wings, a fresh wave of pain erupted within him.

"Oh, fuck," Wash muttered.

"He's coming to." That same deep tenor that had tugged Wash into consciousness spoke again. "Where the hell is Ward?"

"I'm sorry, Master Krispin," a new voice said. "I'm here."

"Stay down, Washington," the tenor ordered—Master Krispin probably. "Let our doc check you over first."

Wash realized someone had a grip on his shoulder and was using it to keep him from rising.

"Is he one of the tolerant, large gargoyles, my beloved?" another voice asked. "Or is he one of the assholes?"

"Um, no," Dloben replied, although he sounded nervous as hell. "Washington never abused us smaller gargoyles. His younger brother is mated with a small human, so . . . well . . ." He hesitated, then finally explained, "I suppose I'd call his actions apathetic. He mostly just ignored us unless he was with his brother, Lionad."

Well, isn't that a stunning endorsement. So that other speaker must have been Dloben's mate, Basques.

And why the fuck do I care?

"I'm awake," Wash grumbled, doing his best to ignore the man—vampire—poking at his back. "What happened?"

"Do you remember fighting with another gargoyle?" the tenor asked, his voice soft, indicating he must be leaning close. "A gray-hided one?"

"Yeah," Wash admitted, hating that he'd been caught unawares. "Been tracking Chasis for the past week. Should have been more—"

"Chasis," Dloben whispered, interrupting. "Here?"

Feeling a tug on his wing, Wash snarled and twisted, only to let the breath out on a hiss. He inhaled deeply, ready to lay into whoever was touching his sensitive appendage without permission. Except, then the aroma of one of the men leaning close filled his lungs.

Wash snapped his eyes open as an appreciative moan escaped his lips.

Damn! Which one smells like that?

"Um, Mister Doctor Guy," Dloben mumbled softly. "I-It's not polite to um . . ."

Dloben continued to murmur words, but Wash couldn't concentrate on them. Instead, arousal slithered through his veins, flooding his groin with heat. It even managed to beat out the pain, which was nice.

The bourgeoning erection might have been ill-timed, however.

"What's that, Dloben?" another man asked.

Wash thought it sounded like the guy called Ward—the doctor, presumably.

Basques answered. "A gargoyle's wings are sensitive." The vampire cleared his throat. "In a sexual way. Best not to touch them without permission, even if they are injured."

To Wash's relief, the hand on his wing disappeared as a low, feral growl filled the air.

Glancing around, Wash craned his neck to survey the group standing around him. He recognized Basques and Dloben, since he'd seen the pair at the clutch house before the vampire had moved Dloben out. The rest . . . he could only guess.

Opening his mouth, Wash took a deep inhale, using the myriad of extra-sensory taste buds on his tongue to test the air. His focus slid to the man with his hand on his shoulder. That was the same guy that had growled and glared at the man who'd been inspecting his back and wing.

"You're my mate." The words were out of Wash's mouth before he could think better of them.

The pale-blue eyes of the man—vampire—in question focused on Wash. He grinned widely, showing off his fangs. "Yes, Washington. I am." Sliding his hand from Wash's shoulder and up his neck, he rumbled, "I'm Krispin Stearling, and it is very nice to meet you." Then his brows lifted, becoming nearly hidden by the slightly sweaty black hair plastered to his forehead. "How long have you been tracking Chasis in my city, and why didn't your chieftain notify me?"

Well, damn . . . put like that.

"Shit," Wash muttered, grimacing. "I missed the sign, too caught up in following Chasis's scent on the wind." Holding Krispin's gaze, he apologized. "I'm sorry for the breach of protocol." Then the name hit Wash. "Oh, fuck! You're the master here, aren't you?"

Krispin nodded, his smile making him appear extremely pleased to have been recognized. "Indeed, I am." With a wink, he added, "Don't worry. I won't get you in trouble with Chieftain Kinsey." Threading his fingers through Wash's hair, Krispin scratched gently at his scalp. "Would never do anything to cause you harm, my beloved Washington."

"Just Wash, please," Wash murmured, pushing into the man's caress. He'd always thought Washington sounded damn pretentious. Except, his movement caused a fresh wave of pain to flare through his back. "Ow."

"We really should get him to the infirmary, Master Krispin," Ward stated, cutting in from his position at Wash's right hip. "Paranormals heal fast, but these claw rakes are deep."

Right. Those.

Except . . . my duty . . .

"I need to follow Chasis," Wash mumbled.

"You will do no such thing," Krispin declared.

"But—" Wash began.

Krispin cut him off with a forefinger to his lips. "Chasis is in rough shape, so he won't have been able to get far," he assured. "And you are my beloved. Now that I've found you, I can't just let you fly off while injured." Grimacing, Krispin grumbled, "I'd prefer you not fly off at all, but I understand duty. Let's get you patched up, Wash." Then he rubbed over his scalp again while saying, "And we have much to discuss."

Wash figured that was all true, although his stomach clenched upon hearing Krispin's comment about not flying off at all. He was a tracker for his clutch. One of the best. His entire point of existence included flying off.

Except, flying off means leaving my mate.

Gargoyles don't leave their mates behind . . . right?

"We'll figure it out," Wash muttered, struggling to focus. The waves of pain radiating through him made his brain feel sluggish.

"Yes, we will," Krispin concurred. "Let's get you up."

As Krispin helped Wash to stand, keeping his arm slung low around his hips to avoid his sensitive back, he finally noticed the blood splattered over the vampire's front. "Are you injured?" He didn't think he could smell the male's blood, but he needed to be sure.

"No, beloved," Krispin replied, urging him along a garden path. "This is your blood, as well as Chasis's."

As they moved, Ward hovered close. Basques had his arm around Dloben, and the pair led a few steps ahead of them. The big vampire kept glancing over his shoulder at them before sweeping his gaze over the sky, clearly searching.

"Chasis's blood?" Wash muttered. "You fought him? And how did you get my blood on you?"

Wash couldn't hide his confusion as the opening doors of an elevator appeared.

What the hell happened?

"Hey, Kris. Just got Basques's message," a large, blond man called as he exited the lift. His light-brown eyes widened as he hustled forward. "Who's this?"

"This is Wash. My beloved," Krispin told him, sounding pleased. "He was attacked by that asshole Chasis and landed in the garden." Squeezing Wash's hip, he continued, "This is my second, Ridger Carruthers."

"Damn, congrats." Ridger grinned broadly as he used a hand to hold the elevator doors open so they could enter. "A beloved falling from the sky. Nice!" Then his expression darkened, and he indicated the blood spray with his free hand. "You okay, though, Master Krispin?"

"I'm fine," Krispin replied. "And I want to go to my suite, Basques." He indicated the panel with floor buttons on it. "I need him in my space."

"Master, I really would recommend a trip to the infirmary first," Ward encouraged as Basques hit one of two buttons on the panel. "His back needs stitches."

15

One button had an up arrow while the second had a down arrow. They went down.

"I was thinking of a much more enjoyable way of healing you, Wash," Krispin told him, giving him a feral smile. "But it would start the bonding process. You game?"

"I, uh . . ." Wash's mind stuttered. "Bonding?"

"Mmm-hmmm." Krispin winked at him. "A vampire's saliva contains a healing agent. It's why donors don't end up with scars." As the doors opened, he explained, "I wish to lay you on my bed, clean your back and wings with my tongue, and prepare you for my cock."

Wash could scent the vampire's arousal, and it called to his own. Groaning, he couldn't resist reaching down and palming his erection. He knew he tented his loincloth obscenely, but there wasn't a damn thing he could do about it.

"We're both paranormals, my beloved," Krispin reminded him. "When we find the other half of our souls, we move fast."

Wash swallowed hard. "Y-Yeah, we do."

But do I want to move this *fast?*

His cock twitched. His body was more than on board with the idea.

"We can start," Wash found himself saying. "But we'll have to talk at some point, too, because . . . well—" He paused and frowned at his mate. "I still have a job to finish."

Krispin narrowed his eyes, his lips pinching. Then he nodded. "Any mating comes with some adjustments. We'll work it out."

Wash nodded.

"Master Krispin, you never did explain the blood," Ridger pointed out.

"Ah, right." Krispin paused before a door. "Keycard is in my left pocket, if you please, Basques."

Basques slid his hand into the indicated pocket, and Wash

couldn't hold in his growl. The move was too intimate.

Oh, wow. Possessive mating urges.

"Relax, my beloved," Krispin crooned. "Basques has only ever been a friend, and he's mated."

"I know," Wash grumbled, scowling as Basques opened the door.

"And to answer your question, Ridger," Krispin began while leading them forward into a spacious suite. "I watched Wash crash in the garden, and as I crossed to him, another gargoyle landed next to him. He slashed his back, spraying blood on me, which told me Wash is my beloved, so I drove the bastard off." Scowling, Krispin added, "If I'd known it was Chasis, I would have incapacitated him, instead."

"Got it," Ridger replied, nodding. "I'll alert our enforcers and send out a couple trackers. See what we can find."

"Good." Krispin paused and peered around at the others. "I'll need a few hours."

Basques grinned. "We won't bother you for anything but an emergency."

"Thank you," Krispin replied.

Ward cocked his head. "Master, are you certain you don't want me to check him over?"

Shaking his head, Krispin told him, "You checked him over upstairs." Then he focused on Wash, concern creasing his handsome features. "Unless you have a head injury? You landed hard."

Wash hesitated, taking stock of himself. While his head did hurt a bit, it was nothing compared to the pain radiating through his back. "Nothing a good orgasm won't cure." The words were out of Wash's mouth before he could think better of them.

Yep. Thinkin' with my dick.

Ridger and Basques laughed. Dloben blushed. Even the doc cracked a smile.

Krispin growled low in his throat. "That I can help with."

Wash's dick twitched as he listened to the sexy sound.

The other men filed out, and the door clicked closed behind them. Krispin urged him through the foyer and through what looked like a large, open-concept space. There was a large lounging area, a dining room, and a kitchen. Everything was appointed in earth tones with dark, masculine furniture.

"I'll give you the dime tour after I take care of your back, my beloved," Krispin told him, moving them toward a hall. "Or feel free to explore. There is nothing here that I would hide from you."

Wash only responded with a nod. He worried if he opened his mouth, only groans of pain would come out. His head was beginning to spin with the continued movement, and he feared he might have a head injury after all.

Krispin pushed open the door at the end of the hall, revealing a spacious master suite done in the same earth tones. He guided him to the massive bed and helped Wash onto it, lying on his stomach. Skimming his hands up Wash's thigh, he massaged lightly, then gripped the ties on his loincloth.

"May I remove this, Wash?"

A shiver of anticipation worked through Wash. He turned his head to eye the vampire who was his mate and was rewarded with an eyeful. Krispin's erection tented his lounging pants, telling Wash his vampire was just as turned on as he was.

My vampire. Huh.

"Yes, please," Wash murmured. "As long as you're going to strip those."

"I do intend to, yes," Krispin replied. "Give me just a minute to wash the blood off me." Then Krispin pulled the ties of the loincloth. "Lift your hips just a little, if you can."

Gritting his teeth, Wash obeyed. In the next instant, his meager covering was tossed onto a nearby chair. His hard erection slid against the soft fabric of the comforter, drawing another moan from him — this one from pleasure.

"A much better sound." Krispin's voice sounded deep with his need. "Be right back."

Wash peeled his eyelids back open, uncertain when he'd closed them. He was glad he did. The view was absolutely stunning as a gorgeously nude Krispin walked toward a half-open door, his hard ass muscles flexing enticingly.

"Do you know I have to fuck you, too, in order to go through molt?" Wash didn't bother raising his voice, knowing the vampire's sensitive hearing would easily pick up his quiet comment.

"I do," Krispin replied from the bathroom.

The sound of running water began, then shut off a couple of seconds later.

Krispin appeared in the doorway, rubbing his body with the cloth, cleaning the blood from the hard planes of his chest. "Never bottomed before," he admitted. Reaching down, he palmed the thick erection jutting from his thin nest of curls. "But you're my beloved. For you, I will." A bead of pre-cum oozed from Krispin's slit. "Whenever you want me, Wash. I am yours, as you are mine."

Wash groaned as he eyed the sexy vampire. His cock twitched against the comforter, and he shifted restlessly. The sensitive flesh of his erection moving along the blanket sent delicious tingles through his body, and he spread his legs a little so he could rock his heavy balls against the fabric.

"Gods, look at you," Krispin muttered as he strode toward the bed, continuing to jack himself. "Gonna clean you up now and make your senses sing."

More than on board with that, Wash muttered, "Yes, please, mate."

Gods above, I found my mate.

CHAPTER THREE

K rispin's shaft ached, and all he wanted to do was slide his erection deep into the ass of the gargoyle sprawled on his bed. Sadly, he knew that would have to wait. Caring for his beloved's injuries came first.

That didn't stop him from grabbing the lube and dropping it on the bed. Nor did it stop him from admiring the sexy male specimen. His beloved was the picture of masculine beauty — all hard muscles and strong lines.

And the wings. Just damn.

When Dloben and Basques had explained that wings were sensitive in a sexual way, Krispin had just about cut Ward's hand off.

Crawling onto the bed, Krispin eased between Wash's spread calves. He rubbed up his thighs, watching the firm globes tense and relax. Easing his gaze higher, he took in the deep, red grooves flaying his back.

His gut clenched, and his mouth watered. The aroma of Wash's blood teased his nostrils.

Delicious.

"Time to heal you, my beloved," Krispin murmured as he leaned over. "Just relax. I'll take care of you."

Krispin received a grunt, but Wash didn't respond with words. He didn't mind. Opening his mouth, he began lapping along the deep slices, using his fingers to gently ease the flesh back together.

As Wash's flavorful, life-giving fluid coated his tongue, Krispin's saliva did exactly as he'd promised. Beneath his slow and careful ministrations, Wash's flesh knitted back together. The wounds sealed and healed.

While Krispin hoped never to see Wash injured in such a way again, he couldn't deny that he was enjoying himself. His cock jerked at his groin, his taste buds sang, and his mouth watered for more. Even his balls began to tingle as he finally worked over the last of the grooves.

Wash panted beneath him, the scent of his arousal thickening.

Krispin pressed a light kiss to Wash's nape, then eased his hips down, resting his erection on his forever lover's crease. "Now your wings," he whispered huskily. "That okay with you?"

Groaning, Wash nodded. "Hell yeah."

As Krispin moved his left hand to Wash's black appendage, stroking the surprisingly soft hide gently, he began rocking his hips. He couldn't help but need stimulation on his engorged shaft. Never could he remember being so hard.

Pleasure filled Krispin as he felt Wash rock his hips, pushing back against him. The wing he fondled twitched and fluttered. Leaning over, Krispin began licking at the small tears there.

Wash groaned loudly, and a shudder worked through his big body. "K-Krispin," he muttered on a panting breath. "Oh, gods."

Loving that response, Krispin continued his ministrations. He rested his full weight on his gargoyle's back and moved his right hand to his beloved's uninjured right wing. Stroking that one too, he licked and healed the other, continuing to lick, touch, and tease even after he saw no more marks.

Krispin felt his heavy balls begin to lift, and he realized he was shockingly close to orgasm. To his pleasure, Wash was right there with him. Between one heartbeat and the next, Krispin felt the hard shudder work through his beloved, and the salty-sweet scent of cum filled the air.

"Wash," Krispin mumbled as his own orgasm slammed through his system.

Unable to help himself, Krispin continued to rut as he marked Wash with his seed. He spurted over and over as his body trembled with the force of his release. His mind floated for several minutes even after his body finally stilled.

Krispin inhaled deeply, slowly, and let it out on a low moan. "Holy shit," he mumbled before rubbing his goatee-covered chin on Wash's back. "That was . . ."

"Yeah," Wash replied, his voice rough. Then he chuckled softly. "Intense."

Gathering a little strength—*damn, when was the last time a frotting session wore me out*—Krispin eased off of Wash. "Stay still," he encouraged as he rubbed his palm over his lover's freshly healed back. "I'll grab a cloth to clean us up." When Wash turned his head and met his gaze, Krispin smirked at him. "Then we'll talk a little, make out like randy teenagers, and begin round two."

To Krispin's pleasure, Wash's deep brown lips curved into a smile and another deep laugh escaped him.

"Sounds good."

Krispin slipped from the bed and headed back to his bathroom. After grabbing and dampening another cloth, he cleaned himself. He rinsed the cloth, grabbed a dry one, and returned to the bed.

Noticing Wash had shifted sideways a little, Krispin lifted a brow. Then he saw the wet spot and grinned. "That's what the dry one is for." He spread the dry one over the soaked comforter before wiping the damp cloth over Wash's back. "Feeling better? Still have an ache in your head?"

Wash's deep rumbling voice went straight to Krispin's balls, and he began thickening again.

"I'm fine now. Thanks to you."

After Krispin finished with Wash's back, he urged him to roll over. Climbing onto the bed again, he hesitated as he took in his gargoyle's wings. "Is it okay to lay on your wings?" Krispin asked curiously before running a bit of damp cloth over his beloved's cock and balls. "Or don't gargoyles cuddle?"

Krispin figured he would feel embarrassed, but this was his beloved. Even though they were similar in height and build, he still wanted to hold the male.

"Yeah. Gargoyles cuddle," Wash told him. "It's fine to lay on my wing." Lifting a hand, he beckoned with his fingers. "C'mere."

Pleased, Krispin closed the distance between them. He settled on his side, the wing beneath him, and curled against Wash. Slotting his body against his beloved's, Krispin slung his left leg over the gargoyle's thighs.

Krispin slid his left hand along Wash's jaw, tracing over the slightly bumpy hide. Leaning close, he pressed his lips to the other man's. To Krispin's pleasure, Wash immediately opened to him.

Sliding his tongue into Wash's mouth, Krispin explored slowly. He savored the man's masculine flavor and the way his longer tongue stroked along his own. Having taken the edge off, he felt no need to rush, even though he'd originally told Wash he planned to fuck him.

We'll get to that.

Krispin felt Wash's hands on him, the skim of his claws over his back, side, and chest. He enjoyed the goose bumps the rasp created, and his nipples beaded pleasantly. Sliding his hand into Wash's thick dark hair, he scratched at the gargoyle's scalp.

After several minutes, Krispin drew the kiss to an end. He peered into his lover's honey-brown eyes, appreciating the way they deepened to the color of good whiskey with his arousal. Krispin didn't need to glance down to know Wash once more sported an erection.

Even with Krispin's own dick in a similar state, he felt no driving need to race to the finish line. His beloved was there, in his arms, in his bed, and he had every intention of keeping him there. They had all the time in the world to explore.

"So," Wash began softly. "How long have you been coven master?"

"Over one-hundred-fifty years," Krispin replied, drifting his hand down over Wash's torso. He rubbed over a nipple. "How long have you been a tracker?"

Wash whistled even as his bud tightened under Krispin's fingertips. "That's a lot for a vampire, right? You all live around five hundred years normally? Did you take it over from someone? Win a fight? Get it from Dad?" After a pause, Wash added, "And I've been a tracker for over three hundred years."

Krispin nodded, feeling his eyebrows lift. "Over three hundred? How old are you?"

"Uh, this'll be my four-hundred-seventeenth summer."

"Damn." Then Krispin remembered another tidbit about gargoyles. "And your kind can live almost two millennia. Guess I'll be a round a while. That'll be nice, since now I won't die on Basques for a while." Sadness filled him for a moment as he commented, "Although the jury's still out on Ridger. Maybe I'll have to send him to all the gargoyle clutches around to see if he'll bond with one, too. I hate the idea of losing my second."

Humming, Wash rubbed down his back. "I figure when a human with family bonds with a paranormal, they think the same thing."

After another nod, Krispin recalled Wash's other questions. He explained how he and his two friends had left their birth coven when a bastard had taken control of it. They'd formed their own coven and had slowly begun accepting members, always careful of who joined.

Krispin shared how he'd only been challenged twice in all the years he'd led.

Sliding his hand downward, Krispin encountered Wash's erection. He finally focused on it and wrapped his fingers around the length. Jacking him slowly, he explored the shaft.

"Damn, you're thick," Krispin commented, guessing him to be about nine inches with a healthy girth. "Gonna require a lot of lube to take this."

Krispin found his hole tightening at just the thought, but his cock twitched, too.

"I'll get you plenty ready," Wash told him. "You'll enjoy it. Promise."

Before Krispin could think up a response, he felt something nudge at his balls, then beyond. Since he still felt the gargoyle's hands on his torso, petting and stroking, he tensed and twisted.

"Relax, my mate," Wash rumbled. "That's my tail."

Krispin spotted the brown appendage rubbing between his legs and snapped his attention back to Wash's face. "Tail?"

Wash nodded. "Oh, yeah." His expression was growing hungry. "I have great control over my tail."

"Damn." Krispin hadn't considered that.

Sliding one hand into Krispin's hair, Wash tightened the other around his waist. He used the hold to ease Krispin back onto his body. "C'mere," he muttered. "Time to play."

Krispin couldn't remember the last time he'd had a lover take charge in the bedroom. To his surprise, he liked it. He enjoyed the way it felt to have Wash pull him across his chest, the way he urged his legs to drape on either side of his thighs, as well as how he guided them through another kiss with one hand.

Wash must have been doing something else with his other hand, since it wasn't on Krispin's body.

When Wash broke the kiss, he held up the lube. "You mentioned ya wanted to fuck me." He wiggled the bottle. "Now or later?" Wash rocked his hips. "'Cause I want someone's dick in someone's ass now."

"You're ready to start bonding?" Krispin's mind scrambled. "You mentioned reservations earlier."

Nodding, Wash admitted, "I'm worried you're gonna be pissed when I tell ya I still plan to finish my clutch's last assignment, but I figured if we started bonding, you'd know I intend to return to ya."

Tension ratcheted through Krispin's body, and it wasn't caused by sexual need that time. He frowned as he peered into the face of his beloved. "You're leaving me?" Krispin mentally winced at how needy that sounded. "Fuck and run, huh?"

Wash growled softly, his brown brow ridges furrowing. "It's not like that, mate, and you know it. I have a job to do."

Even knowing he shouldn't be a dick about it didn't stop his next words. He was used to people following his commands.

"You're aware that since we've started bonding, you're the only one I can drink from, right?" Krispin levered up a bit, straddling Wash's waist. "I'm the master of my coven, Wash. Your place is here. At my side."

"And I will be at your side, Krispin," Wash replied, frowning, rubbing his hand over his hip in an obvious attempt to soothe. "But Chasis has gone rogue. He's a danger to us. I have to track him down and report his whereabouts to my chieftain."

Krispin growled softly, his vision beginning to haze. "Kinsey will no longer be your chieftain," he snarled, leaning close again until their faces were only inches apart. "You'll be part of this coven. My coven. Where I am master."

Wash lifted his head and pecked a kiss to his lips. "Yes. I

understand that. But duty first, my mate."

"If anything were to happen to you, I—" Krispin stopped and swallowed hard. Allowing his eyelids to slide closed, he forced himself to admit, "I can't lose you now that I've just found you, Wash."

To Krispin's surprise, Wash rolled them. A second later, he was on his back—the other man sprawled over him, sliding his fingers into his hair.

Krispin felt his heart lurch when he took in the understanding expression on Wash's face.

"You won't lose me, Krispin," Wash assured him, his tone sounding deep and gentle. A smile toyed at the corners of his lips. "Regardless of how we met, I don't make a habit of running into those I'm tracking. I call in the enforcers, and they take down the rogue."

"Then how did that fluke happen?" Krispin asked softly, staring up at his mate.

Even with the tough conversation, Krispin's erection didn't wane in the least. He figured it was because of being manhandled. Krispin rather enjoyed it.

"I smelled Dloben and realized their scent trails were intermingled," Wash revealed. "His was fainter, and I realized Chasis was zeroing in on the male." Grimacing, he shook his head. "I was planning to find Dloben and warn him, so I left Chasis's trail . . . or thought I did. Evidently, he'd been sitting on a nearby building watching the sky, probably waiting to see if Dloben would reappear. He just happened to spot me, instead." Shaking his head, Wash added, "It's a good learning lesson. I won't let that happen again."

Krispin let out a long breath. He realized he needed to let this go. He couldn't force his mate to stay with him. In fact, Krispin admired Wash's insistence on finishing a job.

"Okay," Krispin replied softly, rubbing his hands up and

down Wash's back. "I apologize for"—he winced—"behaving like an ass."

Wash shook his head as he smiled down at him. "Not an ass. A worried lover." Dipping his head, he pecked a kiss to Krispin's lips. "I kinda like it."

Growling softly, Krispin wrapped his leg around Wash's waist. He bucked and twisted while gripping his shoulders and shoving. With his vampire strength, he quickly reversed their positions.

Krispin grinned down at his smirking lover. "You let me do that, didn't you?" he guessed.

Wash shrugged. "I'll never resist my mate manhandling me."

"That's not a no," Krispin countered with a scoff. "Just for that, I'm going to fuck you first."

"I'm more than okay with that," Wash replied, a hungry light filling his amber eyes. "Make me yours."

Krispin grabbed the tube of lube that Wash had dropped at some point. "You're already mine, beloved." Scooting backward, he used his knee to urge Wash to spread his legs. "This is just a formality."

"Playtime," Wash countered.

"Getting to know each other." Krispin poured a dollop of lube onto his fingers. "Teasing and touching."

The way Wash easily spread his legs wide, Krispin felt his anticipation ramp up. His cock throbbed, ready for more. Rubbing his fingertips along the groove of Wash's thigh, Krispin lowered the wet fingers of his other hand to his lover's hole.

"How about sucking?" Wash asked.

Then his breathing hitched as Krispin rubbed at his opening, teasing and touching, just as he'd said.

Krispin felt his heart rate spike upon seeing and feeling that response from his lover. The bead of pre-cum oozing from Wash's thick erection made his mouth water. More than happy to give his beloved what he wanted, he lowered his head.

As Krispin pushed one finger deep into his lover, he opened his mouth and swiped his tongue over the gargoyle's wide crown, teasing his way under his foreskin.

Delicious!

CHAPTER FOUR

Wash let out a long, low groan as he watched Krispin wrap his lips around his cock. When he'd asked if his mate sucked, he hadn't really thought he would. The vampire was the master of his coven, the leader, the boss, the guy who called all the shots.

Their argument from seconds before had made it abundantly clear that Krispin expected to get his way.

And now he's sucking me like a goddamned hoover, and it feels fan-fucking-tastic!

Krispin knew his way around a cock. He teased at his foreskin, massaged his frenulum, and sucked strongly on the upstroke. He even deep throated and swallowed around his crown. His tongue remained in motion, tracing along his shaft with each move.

Wash felt the finger in his ass become two, then three, but he never felt the stretch or burn. His mate kept him too on edge. His balls began to tighten, and he felt the tell-tale tingle at the base of his spine.

When Wash's thighs started to tremble and his abs tightened, he moaned roughly and tugged on Krispin's hair. "Now," he pleaded. "God, in me now."

Releasing his erection with a slurp, Krispin grinned lewdly at him through swollen, gleaming lips. "Not God," he teased as he pulled his fingers free of Wash's channel. "But probably close."

Barking a laugh, Wash shook his head. He couldn't remember the last time he'd enjoyed sex so much. Of course, this was his mate, so he supposed it made sense.

"About to come," Wash whispered, watching raptly as Krispin coated his length with slick. "Want you inside me when I do."

"Want that, too," Krispin admitted. Levering over him, he pressed his crown to Wash's readied hole. "Push out, my beloved."

Wash did.

Instantly, his ring stretched, admitting Krispin into his body.

Krispin pushed and pushed, sinking deep in one long, smooth glide. His vampire paused with his erection buried deep inside him. He rested his left hand on the comforter beside Wash's head and gripped his thigh with his right hand, urging him to lift his leg.

"Gods, you do feel amazing, my gargoyle," Krispin whispered. Dipping his head, he pressed a lingering kiss to Wash's lips. "Love the feel of your walls encasing me."

Wash groaned as he tightened and relaxed his chute muscles. "Yessss," he hissed, wrapping his arms around his mate. "Feel so good in me."

Groaning, Krispin shuddered above him.

"Need to move," his vampire muttered. "Please tell me I can move."

"Hell yeah," Wash replied, surprised the vampire had asked permission. "Wanna feel ya for days."

"You will," Krispin assured.

Then Krispin began to move. He eased his hips backward slowly. Once his crown teased at Wash's ring, he reversed direction, pushing in again. Krispin repeated the move slowly several times, obviously getting a feel for him.

Wash groaned, rubbing up and down his spine with one hand. With his other, he threaded it into his hair. "Faster," he pleaded, peering into his vampire's blue eyes, eyes darkened with lust. "Please."

Growling low in his throat, Krispin grinned. "Yes, be-loved."

Krispin tightened his hold on Wash's thigh as his irises bled red. A feral gleam entered his eyes, and his hips sped up. His balls slapped into Wash's ass as he began pounding his hole.

Moaning, Wash wrapped his free leg around Krispin's waist and rocked into each move. His mate pegged his prostate over and over, sending fiery sparks through his rectum. His balls pulled tight as his orgasm bowled through his system. Wash called out Krispin's name as he coated both their stomachs and chests with spurt after spurt of cum.

"Mine!" Krispin snarled as he snapped his head forward and sank his fangs into Wash's flesh.

Wash gasped, only to let the air out on a groan of pure bliss. Ecstasy coursed through his system. His balls tightened once more, and another orgasm rocked through his body, the sucking pulls on his neck transferring straight to his groin.

When Krispin eased his teeth out of Wash's flesh and licked over it, Wash sighed with pleasure. He registered the heat in his chute and hummed happily, knowing he'd pleased his mate. Grinning, Wash figured the expression looked a little loopy, but he didn't care.

Rubbing his hands up and down Krispin's spine, Wash held his lover close. He enjoyed the weight of the man on his body. His vampire gently released his leg, so he placed both back on the bed, but he tightened his arms, encouraging Krispin to stay in place.

Krispin kissed his neck, then turned his head a little so their gazes met. His eyes were once again blue, and he sported a satisfied expression.

Wash felt about the same, but he knew they weren't done, yet.

Smirking, Wash reached over and picked up the lube. "Open it," he ordered, holding it up.

Even as Krispin arched one black brow, he did as he was told.

When the vampire began to ease back, Wash tightened his arm again. "No. Stay." He squeezed him until he felt his mate settle.

"You're a bit bossy in bed," Krispin commented, but he didn't sound upset.

Wash shrugged once. "A bit." Then he poured a healthy dollop of the slick on the last several inches of his tail. "We're gonna make out with your dick still in my ass while I open you up with my tail. You good with that?"

Krispin's brows shot up, and a wide grin stretched his lips. "You have that much control?"

"I do." Wash waggled his eyebrow ridges. "I've fucked myself with my tail more times than I can count. Better than any dildo."

Tipping his chin in a silent acknowledgment, Krispin chuckled. "Okay."

After closing the cap with his thumb, Wash threaded his fingers into Krispin's hair. He brought their lips together. Opening his mouth, he teased his tongue against his vampire's, pleased when he immediately opened to him.

As Wash made out with Krispin, mapping his mouth in languorous strokes, he skimmed his tail along his vampire's crease. Reaching his lover's hole, he broke the kiss only long enough to whisper, "Spread your legs a little." Then he captured Krispin's mouth again.

Feeling Krispin shift above him, Wash smiled against the other man's lips. As he eased his tail into his mate's chute, maybe just an inch or so, he wondered if the vampire realized how obedient he was. Wash would never ask, but he figured it had to do with him wanting to please his beloved.

Works for me.

For the next ten minutes, Wash made out with Krispin as he fucked him with his tail. He knew from personal experience how good it felt. His appendage was warm and malleable, and he had excellent control over it.

Each time Wash rubbed over his vampire's prostate, the man trembled in his grip. He moaned into his mouth, and Wash happily accepted every noise he made. Wash felt Krispin's cock harden within the confines of his body, and he began repeatedly squeezing his mate's cock with his chute muscles.

Finally, Krispin broke the kiss on a groan. He pressed his forehead into the crook of Wash's shoulder and began to rut. His vampire trembled in his hold, whispering Wash's name along with a litany of grunts, groans, mines, and beloveds.

Wash's own cock throbbed between them, hot and heavy. His balls filled again, and it took every damn ounce of self-control not to allow himself to fly over that edge again. He planned to come in his mate, instead.

To that end, Wash began rubbing his tail over Krispin's prostate even harder.

His back arching, a look of pleasure-pained bliss creasing his features, Krispin threw back his head and roared.

Wash felt Krispin's seed pour into his channel as his vampire's cock throbbed and twitched within him. He hummed his enjoyment, loving the sensation of being marked within. As Wash held his lover, who trembled in his hold, he waited patiently for Krispin to gather himself just a little.

After several minutes, Krispin turned his head and pressed a kiss to his neck. "Holy fuck, Wash," he muttered roughly. "Never felt anything like that."

"Not done quite, yet, mate," Wash murmured huskily. "I'm gonna roll us, okay?"

Krispin nodded. "Mmm-kay. 'Cause I don't think I can move on my own."

Wash grinned, pleased by that comment. Then he gently eased Krispin to the side and rolled them, still keeping his tail in his vampire's chute. Once Wash hovered over him, he threaded his fingers in his mate's thick black locks.

"First time is easiest on your stomach." As Wash made the comment, he figured Krispin already knew that. "I'd love to see your face, but it's up to you."

Rubbing his hands up and down Wash's neck, Krispin smiled sluggishly. "Like this, my beloved."

Nodding, Wash complied. He grabbed a pillow and eased it under Krispin's hips before gently removing his tail. Then he grabbed the lube and poured it onto his straining erection. After a quick couple of jacks, coating himself, Wash guided his cock to Krispin's hole.

Wash rested his weight on his left hand near Krispin's torso, then pressed steadily. Unable to help himself, he watched his flared crown stretch his lover's hole. Then he was inside, and rippling hot pressure encased his crown.

Krispin's hiss yanked Wash's gaze to his vampire's face. He spotted the lines of tension there and immediately set out to soothe them. Rubbing his other hand up and down his vampire's torso, he plucked at his nipples and teased along the lines of his abdominals as well at the grooves of his groin. All the while, Wash managed to keep his hips still.

Gods, though, was it tough.

After taking a deep breath, Krispin let it out slowly. Then he lifted his arms and settled his hands on Wash's biceps.

"Push, my beloved," Krispin encouraged. "It's not bad. I want you."

"Can you relax just a little?" Wash asked, lowering his head and nibbling at Krispin's neck where he longed to sink in his canines. "Take another couple of slow breaths for me, my mate."

Krispin complied as he rubbed his hands up to grip Wash's

neck. "Come here," he urged, tightening his grip. "Kiss me."

Happy to be the one obeying, Wash closed the distance between them. One thing he enjoyed about Krispin was his penchant for kissing—and he kissed fantastically. His mouth should be considered a lethal weapon the way he moved it against Wash's own.

Fortunately, the activity also seemed to distract Krispin from the discomfort.

Within just a few heartbeats, Wash felt the stranglehold on his cock head ease. He took that as the sign it was, his mate's body accepting his intrusion, and began to move. After pushing forward a little, Wash retreated.

Over and over, Wash slowly buried his length within the confines of Krispin's body. His mate was so hot, so perfect, that by the time Wash felt his balls nuzzle the vampire's crack, they were pulled high and tight. He realized he was going to come embarrassingly fast.

That's okay. We have centuries to work on our stamina.

With that thought in mind, Wash broke the kiss. He began licking and nipping his way along Krispin's jaw, then down his neck, as he slowly began to rut deep into his mate, again and again. He didn't try to stop his orgasm from cresting. He wanted to come inside his vampire, marking the man inside and out.

With a low groan, Wash's orgasm rolled over him. He buried his erection deep and poured his fluid into the vampire. His hips twitched as a shudder worked through him, bliss pinging throughout his system.

After placing one more licking kiss to the flesh where Krispin's neck met his shoulder, Wash bit. He sank his canines deep into the man and sucked hard. His mate's life-giving fluid flowed into his mouth.

To Wash's pleasure, Krispin's cry of delight filled the room. His vampire's body shook beneath him. His chute rippled around his still spurting length, milking him for another couple of bursts. The delicious scent of Krispin's seed intensified, and the warmth coated their abdominals.

Wash eased his teeth out of Krispin's flesh, then quickly licked across the wound. After sealing it, he stared at his claiming mark. A satisfaction he'd never before experienced coiled in his belly.

Mine!

"You look like the cat that ate the canary," Krispin murmured, his voice rough. He teased along the back of Wash's neck. "Good look on you."

Meeting Krispin's gaze, Wash smiled. "I just claimed my mate, so . . . yeah. I'm doing pretty good here."

Krispin chuckled. "Me, too." Then he winced and peered down. "And we are so coated in seed that I feel it dripping down my sides." A rough snort escaped the man. "New feeling for me."

"Do you have a jetted tub or something? A soaker tub, at least?" Wash eased up, slipping his overly sensitive softening prick from his mate's body. "It'd be good for your ass right about now."

Nodding, Krispin revealed, "It's even large enough to accommodate us both."

Wash hummed appreciatively and slipped off the bed.

When Krispin did the same, he winced, his discomfort apparent.

The need to take care of his mate surged through him. "Come on, Krispin." He wrapped his arm around his vampire's shoulders. "Let's get you settled."

"Wanna share a bottle of wine in the tub with me?" Krispin asked, wrapping his arm around Wash's waist. "And we'll continue chatting?"

Liking that idea, Wash nodded. "Perfect."

"I'll get the wine," Krispin told him, pulling away. "Did you need food? I have some finger foods in the fridge."

"I could eat," Wash revealed. He rarely turned down food.

Krispin turned toward the doorway. "Start the tub. I'll be back in a minute." Then his gaze strayed to the bed, and he snickered. "Damn. That comforter is a total loss."

Turning his attention to the bed, Wash let out a laugh of his own. There were multiple wet spots, a puddle where lube had spilled, and plenty of tiny dots where something slick had dripped. A couple of the darker spots could even have been blood.

"Naw, it'll all come out," Wash countered, teasing. Then he cradled Krispin's nape and drew him in for a short kiss. "Hurry back."

Nodding, Krispin drew away while winking. "Bossy beloved."

Growing serious, Wash assured, "I'll always defer to you around others."

Krispin dipped his head. "Thank you."

Then Krispin left the room.

Wash stayed where he was for a moment, watching Krispin leave, the gorgeous view once again catching his attention.

Gods, my mate is a sexy man.

Once Krispin disappeared, Wash headed into the bathroom. He whistled under his breath upon seeing the corner soaker tub. Just as his vampire had stated, it was large enough to fit two people.

A wave of jealousy surged through him as he thought of how many people Krispin had shared it with.

Then Wash rolled his eyes—*Dumb thought. I'm over four hundred years old*—and he started the tub.

CHAPTER FIVE

K rispin growled low in his throat, glaring at the vampire sitting before him. "You almost drained that human dry with your *enthusiasm*, Gerard."

Placing his palms on his desk, Krispin leaned over the wood. Good thing it separated them, or he would have his hands wrapped around the asshole's throat. As it was, he barely managed to keep his claws from extending.

"Explain!"

At least the dark-haired vampire had the good sense to look sheepish.

Gerard hunched his shoulders and stared at the ground. Then he had to go and ruin it by muttering, "She ended up being okay, and her mind was wiped. It's all fine."

Ridger, who happened to be sitting beside Gerard, reached over and cuffed him upside the head. His second had been the one to discover Gerard in the bathroom of the hotel with his . . . donor. The woman had been pale, her eyes glazed — and not with passion — her exposed breasts heaving, and her skirt rucked up around her waist as Gerard sank his cock into her over and over. All the while, Gerard had been sucking greedily at the vein in her neck.

If Ridger hadn't walked in at that exact moment, Krispin feared Gerard would have killed her. As it was, his second had ordered the other vampire to release her neck, which he'd done. Then Gerard had thrown his head back and groaned, coming inside her. Gerard had sighed, grinned, and pulled out of her . . . and not a condom in sight.

Gerard also hadn't sealed the bite wound.

Ridger had felled him with one punch, sealed the bite wound himself, then helped the half-comatose lady right her clothes. His second had contacted Enforcer Pierce and Enforcer Carmine. He'd ordered them to take Gerard to Krispin while carrying the woman to the infirmary.

They would have to keep an eye on her—Jasmine, according to her driver's license—to make certain she didn't end up pregnant, even with the pills she'd had in her purse.

Frowning, leaning away from Ridger, Gerard scowled. "I just waited too long between feedings, Master Krispin," he whined, meeting his gaze. "I was hungry, and she tasted so good, and"—once again, he rolled one shoulder in a *no biggie* way—"she wanted it raw, anyway. She's the one who said don't worry about a condom, and I'm a paranormal, so not like I could get anything even if she did have something."

"On your application, you claimed to be over one hundred years old. That was over two decades ago, Gerard." Master Krispin ground out his words, anger simmering within him. "This is the *fourth* incident in the last six months. What the fuck is going on with you?"

Krispin truly didn't get it. The low-ranking vampire had been a model coven-member for decades. Then he'd started this shit. While Krispin seethed that someone from his coven had nearly killed a human, he knew some of his anger and frustration stemmed from only communicating with Wash through sporadic texts over the last two days.

Fear for his gargoyle permeated him, but he had to keep it carefully in check so no one outside his inner circle found out.

For a long moment, Gerard just stared sullenly at the floor.

That was fine. Krispin could wait. Leaning back in his chair, Krispin crossed his arms over his chest. He peered at the vampire with narrowed eyes.

Finally, just as Krispin knew he would, Gerard cracked. A

deep sigh rattled from his chest. He rubbed at his pectoral in the vicinity of his heart.

"She wasn't my beloved, but I loved her," Gerard muttered, blinking quickly. "But then she moved on, and I"—he cleared his throat and shifted restlessly in his chair—"I intend to find a donor, but then I start thinking about her, and I walk away, until the craving for blood gets so bad it's all I can think about. Then *that* sometimes happens. I lose control." Resting his elbows on his thighs, Gerard placed his head in his hands. "And I feel like shit."

Damn. That's not what I expected.

"We've all nursed broken hearts at one time or another," Ridger commented softly after exchanging a glance with Krispin. He reached over and rested his hand on Gerard's shoulder. "It sucks, and I know this isn't what you wanna hear, but I'm gonna say it anyway. It'll pass. It'll get better."

Gerard lifted his head and peered at Ridger with red-rimmed eyes. "When?" His voice broke on that one word.

Krispin felt a pang in the vicinity of his own heart, and suddenly, he wanted to hear Wash's voice in the worst way.

I'll have to text him after this meeting.

"It's different for everyone," Krispin told his fellow vampire. Rising, he rounded his desk and sat in a chair on Gerard's opposite side. Gripping the other male's upper arm, Krispin squeezed lightly, offering comfort. "What I do know, is now that I'm aware of the problem, we can help."

"How?" Gerard looked so damn confused. On a hundred and twenty-seven-year-old vampire, it wasn't a good look. "It doesn't change anything. She's still not my beloved, and she still moved on because I couldn't commit to her."

"It means," Krispin began. "Now we know why you're having a problem, and we can help you find a donor." Cocking his head, he asked, "If you're not interested in a connection, you could try feeding from a man instead of waiting until you're desperate enough to fuck any female." He spotted

41

the widening of Gerard's eyes and the tell-tale blush. Smirking, Krispin continued, "And we can also get bagged blood if you're really having a tough time. It'll at least tide you over so you don't gorge or run the risk of bloodlust."

"I'm, uh"—Gerard paused and cleared his throat—"never been with a guy. Don't know if I could, um—" He paused and scowled.

"It's not like we don't have regular male donors, either," Ridger pointed out. Their coven didn't have but a handful, all part-time employees at their hotel, but they had a few. "They wouldn't expect you to fuck 'em if you didn't want to. Plus, they'd still orgasm, so they'd enjoy it."

Gerard's eyebrows furrowed, but he began to nod. He also began to look a bit more relaxed. "O-Okay." His smile seemed a little wan, but it was there. "Thank you, and I-I'm so sorry."

Finally, the vampire sounded sincere.

Krispin nodded, squeezed his upper arm once more, then released him. "We all make mistakes. Comes with having a beating heart." Rising, Krispin headed back around his desk. "I'm going to put you on kitchen dishwasher duty for a month," he warned. "Can't allow others to think that shit is acceptable if it were to get out."

So far, the inner circle and the doc knew, but better safe than sorry.

Gerard's head bobbed. "Yes, Master Krispin. I understand." After another nod from him, Gerard left his office.

Krispin picked up his phone and fired off a text to Wash. It was during the day, but since his beloved had gone through molt the morning after their bonding, he knew there was a possibility that he would be awake. A gargoyle gained a human form which they could change into at will. They still had to sleep as a stone statue—something they called roosting—at least once a week, but they could choose that time as long as they didn't wait too long.

Thinking of you. How's the hunt going?

After putting his phone down, Krispin lifted his gaze and spotted a smirking Ridger lounging in his chair.

"What?" Krispin narrowed his eyes at his friend. "Something going on?"

"Naw," Ridger replied, shaking his head. "Bonded looks good on you, even though I know you're worried about him." His brows creased. "How'd Chieftain Kinsey take learning he was losing another gargoyle to us?"

Krispin chuckled as he thought back to that conversation. After Wash had taken care of him in the tub for a while—which had been amazing—they'd curled up in bed together and called the man who would soon be Wash's ex-chieftain. Due to his heightened hearing, Krispin had been able to hear both sides of Wash's conversation.

"After Kinsey greeted Wash and asked how the tracking was going, my beloved explained where he was and why." Krispin smiled as he met his buddy's gaze. "First, he confirmed that Wash was okay. Then he asked how he'd healed so quickly." To Krispin's surprise, he felt his neck begin to heat a little, but he fought it back. "When Wash explained that he found his beloved in a vampire, Kinsey congratulated him and asked if he was bringing him or her to the clutch after he told the enforcers where Chasis was. He also said he was going to contact me to request permission for his enforcers to enter my territory."

"And, of course, you were listening the whole time," Ridger commented, chortling.

"Of course," Krispin confirmed. "Wash told Kinsey that I was in the room with him, that I was his mate, and that he didn't think it'd be possible for me to join his clutch." The fight he was having against his neck warming failed, and he knew he was beginning to blush a bit considering the amused smile curving his friend's lips. "Then Chieftain Kinsey cursed a few times and grumbled about how next time a couple of our people mate, the vampire has to join his clutch, instead."

Ridger barked a laugh, a wide grin splitting his lips. "Sounds about right when you steal one of his best trackers. How is—"

The chime of Krispin's phone interrupted. Picking it up, he couldn't stop his smile.

A snort escaped his second before he stated, "That must be him."

Krispin didn't bother to dignify that was a response. As he flipped his buddy the bird, he opened his phone. His heart warmed as he read the message.

Chasis is still in the city. The scent trails go everywhere, but I'm narrowing down his possible places of roost. Can I swing by to see you for a couple of hours? Lunch? A quickie?

A grin split Krispin's lips as he typed out a response.

As if you even need to ask. When will you get here?

Krispin suddenly felt like a teenage girl with her first crush.

A forty-minute cab ride. Uh . . . can you pay the fare when I arrive?

Even from just the words, Krispin knew the uncertainty and embarrassment Wash had to be feeling.

Of course, beloved. Text when you're a couple minutes out, and I'll meet you out front.

Krispin figured Wash hadn't bothered carrying money on him, since he'd entered the city as an unmated gargoyle. No way would he have any reason to interact with humans. That meant no need for money.

Thank you.

Grinning, Krispin lifted his focus from his phone to discover Ridger still in his seat. His expression had morphed from a shit-eating, teasing grin, to something else. There was a wistfulness in his expression that Krispin completely understood.

"You'll find him or her," Krispin murmured, causing Ridger to blink.

Ridger sucked in a quick breath, then nodded. "How's his hunt going?" he asked instead of addressing his thoughts.

Krispin didn't question the subject change. "He says there are a few places that Chasis could be roosting in the area, but he's taking a break to join me for a meal."

Hopefully, more than just a meal.

"He'll be here in about forty."

Grimacing, Ridger pointed out, "Uh, you have that lunch meeting with Mayor Bickerman in a little over an hour."

"Damn it," Krispin grumbled. "The one I already rescheduled twice because meeting with her is always a hassle." After seeing Ridger nod, he rose to his feet. "Well, then I guess I'm going to be introducing Bickerman to my partner, and if her skanky, bigoted ass has a problem with it, best to know now."

Scoffing, Ridger rose to his feet. "As if she won't do much more than make sour faces and continue to hit on you. She wants your money too much."

"She wants me, too, since you recall her advances during our last meeting," Krispin reminded his friend, who also rose. "Let's head to the kitchens and confirm an extra plate for the meal."

They headed out of Krispin's office, and he locked the door behind him.

Thirty minutes later, having confirmed another place setting and food for the meal, Krispin received a text from his beloved. Instead of Ridger flanking him as he headed through his hotel's front doors, Enforcer Carmine joined him. His second had received a call from a supplier that he'd needed to take.

It wasn't that Krispin couldn't handle himself if something happened, but being the owner of the largest and most popular hotel in the city created a different set of enemies. Any time he walked out the door, he had someone with him. Precaution had kept him alive more than once.

Krispin surveyed the busy streets, enjoying the small-town feel mixed with newer businesses. There were enough quaint shops to bring in tourists plus enough chain stores, coffee shops, and entertainment joints to satisfy just about any type of visitor. After a long day of hiking in the woods, some visitors would dress to the nines and go to a fancy restaurant to restore all those burned calories.

Each time a cab pulled up, Krispin felt a thrill of anticipation.

Carmine chuckled softly from where she stood next to him. Sporting sunglasses, she discreetly surveyed the area. "It's good to see you like this, Master," she murmured, her voice soft and low, only reaching his ears. She still wasn't looking at him. "It does our coven good to see members finally finding beloveds. Offers hope."

Krispin nodded. "Indeed."

Then he spotted another cab, and his heartrate once again spiked. When it stopped a few feet away, he saw the door open, and his gorgeous beloved emerged. He strode purposefully forward, eyes only for the male who appeared to be a slender African American, but he knew was so much more.

Unmindful of who was around, Krispin cupped Wash's nape with one hand while wrapping his other arm around his waist. In human form, Wash had lost a couple of inches. As he dipped his head and pressed his lips to his beloved's, he didn't mind at all.

Any way I can get him.

To Krispin's pleasure, he felt Wash's arms wrap around his waist and hold on tight as he met Krispin's kiss with one of his own. Two days had been two days too long. He couldn't help but probe Wash's depths, and his cock went ramrod straight in his suit slacks.

Suddenly, the honking of a car horn brought Krispin back to where they stood. He broke the kiss and chuckled huskily. Seeing Wash sporting an answering grin, he glanced around and noticed Carmine was paying off the cabbie.

Good.

Keeping his arm around Wash, Krispin started them toward the front door. "Missed you," he murmured, dipping his head to peck another kiss to his temple.

"Missed you, too."

CHAPTER SIX

Wash knew right away that Mayor Tiffany Bickerman didn't like him. The jealousy rolling off the woman was cloying enough to make him want to lean away from her. If he and Krispin hadn't already finished their bond, he would have been pissed each and every time the woman laid a hand on his lover's arm, hand, or shoulder.

As it was, Wash only felt sorry for Krispin. His poor vampire master was doing the best he could to be cordial. His mate's scent, however, screamed disgust . . . and Mayor Bickerman—*oh, please, call me Tiffany*—had only arrived fifteen minutes before.

One of Krispin's vampires had ushered Tiffany and her two assistants into the large, private dining area where Krispin, Wash, Ridger, Basques, and a clearly uncomfortable Dloben had waited. She'd hurried forward, hands outstretched as she greeted Krispin by his name as if they were old friends. When his vampire lover had taken her hand, she'd clasped her second around it, then leaned forward in an obvious attempt to peck his cheek.

Krispin had placed his second hand on Tiffany's shoulder and pushed her back gently. "Oh, easy, there, Mayor Bickerman," he said gently, playing it as if she'd slightly lost her balance and he was helping to right her. "It's good to see you again." Then Krispin had stepped backward.

Tiffany hadn't released him. It was then she'd urged him to call her by her first name. Then she'd reminded him of the two assistants.

Wash hadn't bothered to log their names in his memory. If he had to interact with them in the future, he would, but right then, it seemed to be unnecessary information. Instead, he'd moved forward and rested his hand on Krispin's lower back, silently offering support.

Krispin had seemed to appreciate it, for he'd turned a smile upon him. "And I'd like you to meet my fiancé, Washington soon-to-be Stearling." He winked at Wash, finally managing to pull away from Tiffany, since she seemed in shock. Wrapping his arm around Wash's waist, Krispin stated, "I finally convinced him to make an honest man out of me a couple of nights ago."

Wash chuckled softly as he held out his hand to Tiffany. "Nice to meet you, Mayor."

Tiffany's eyes narrowed as she glanced between them. Since etiquette deemed it, she took his hand. It was the shortest handshake of his life.

Then Tiffany immediately refocused on his vampire. "Krispin, I didn't realize you were . . . bisexual."

Wash just bet she'd intended to say something else and had barely caught herself in time.

"Indeed," Krispin replied simply. Then he indicated the others in the room. "You remember my business partners, Ridger and Basques. And this is Dloben, Basques's husband."

Tiffany didn't bother offering her hand, and none of them did, either. "Of course." She cast a narrow-eyed gaze Dloben's way, but that was all. Smiling at Krispin again, Tiffany asked, "So how long have you and" — she dipped a hand to indicate Wash, but didn't say his name — "been seeing each other?"

Krispin chuckled. "Not nearly long enough, and I'm looking forward to a few more decades." He turned and used his free hand to indicate the oval table. "Please. Join me. My chef is cooking risotto. I understand it's one of your favorites."

"Oh, yes," Tiffany responded, moving closer to him. She

made a play to grab Krispin's arm, as if she expected him to escort her. "So nice of you to remember my favorites, Krispin."

Unable to contain his need to stake his claim, Wash cut in, "Yes, my fiancé has a fantastic memory for detail." As he spoke, he touched Krispin's jaw, causing his vampire to turn his head and focus on him. "One of your many amazing qualities."

Smiling down at him, Krispin murmured, "Thank you, my beloved."

While the move didn't stop Tiffany from sliding her hand into the crook of Krispin's left arm, her face did take on a pinkish hue. Then she cleared her throat loudly. "Well, yes, that's why we appreciate all your generosity, Krispin."

"I'm always happy to help the city," Krispin responded benevolently.

Krispin guided everyone to the table. After encouraging Tiffany into a seat, he took the one next to it, and Wash sat on his other side. Tiffany's two assistants were on her other side, while the rest of the inner circle filled in the rest of the seats.

Immediately, a server appeared and began offering several choices to fill their glasses.

Wash listened carefully, although he didn't contribute much. He found it fascinating that when the town couldn't come up with the funding for a new park, Krispin had stepped up. His mate had offered a sizable donation with strict orders on how the funds could be used.

Apparently, an outdoor amphitheater was being put in at the edge of town. There would be picnic pavilions as well as play areas for children. The location also backed up to the forest, so hiking trails were going to be cut—ones easy for a family with young children. Information plaques would be added along the way, so it would be an educational opportunity.

"I'm always happy to help better our town," Krispin told

Tiffany as she once more simpered about how grateful she was.

Wash barely managed to keep from gagging.

By the time dessert rolled around—a delicious lemon soufflé—Wash decided that he was going to drag his mate to the closest shower, so he could wipe the smell of Tiffany's perfume off his man.

"So, what do you do, Wash?"

Hearing his name, Wash focused on one of the assistants.

"Do you work here at the hotel?" the human continued.

Wash shook his head. "I'm a tracker." Then he realized how that would sound to a human. "Uh, I specialize with missing persons, locating stalkers, or missing merchandise."

"So you're with the police?" the friendly man asked.

Geez, how do I dig myself out of this one?

Wash had rarely interacted with humans in the past, for obvious reasons, and he glanced at Krispin, hoping for help.

"He worked out of a precinct in Chicago for the last decade," Krispin lied smoothly. "A private consultant with them." Resting his hand over Wash's where it rested on the table, Krispin smiled warmly at him. "I've finally convinced him to move here, so he's still considering options."

"Unemployed then?" Tiffany hummed in an unflattering way, clearly expressing what she thought of him—a gold-digging mooch. "Chicago? How could you possibly have met?"

Once again, Krispin saved him. "Wash was on a child abduction case that brought him to this area." Lifting their hands, he pressed a kiss to the back of it. "So glad it did, darling."

"Me, too," Wash responded.

Beyond Krispin, Wash spotted Tiffany's clear look of disapproval.

Yep, probably going to cause trouble. Oh well. Not like the human can do anything.

"So, now that lunch is concluded, would you like to head

to the conference room to go over the plans for the park?" Krispin asked. He indicated his second. "Ridger can show you the way."

Even as everyone began rising, Krispin remained seated. His squeeze to Wash's hand urged him to do the same, so he did.

Standing beside her chair, Tiffany frowned down at them. "I was under the impression that you would be showing us the plans personally."

Krispin shook his head. "My apologies, Tiffany. I had an unexpected issue come up that can't be put off any longer." He pointed at Ridger and Basques. "My business partners know all the details, though. You're in good hands."

Tiffany looked like she wanted to protest.

Fortunately, Ridger took one for the team and offered her a charming smile. "Allow me to escort you, Tiffany." He held out his arm.

For a second, Wash thought she would make a scene. Then she acquiesced and slid her hand into the crook of his elbow.

Ridger glanced back and winked as he began leading her away.

Basques placed a peck on Dloben's lips, then whispered, "I'll be up when I can."

Dloben nodded. He left through a different door.

Once everyone else had cleared the room, Krispin turned and focused on Wash. "Do you have any idea how happy I am to have met you. That woman is a menace." He smirked as he added, "Now I have a legitimate reason to continue refusing her advances. Gods."

Wash laughed softly as he shook his head. It was funny . . . sort of. "She's certainly persistent." Then he rose and tugged Krispin with him. "So, what came up that you needed to get away for?"

"This," Krispin growled, angling their bodies together. He

tugged Wash close, wrapping his arms around him. Dipping his head, Krispin captured Wash's lips in a plundering kiss.

Opening instantly, Wash welcomed his lover's tongue. He fed him a few moans of his own as they teased each other's mouths. Wash relished the flavor of his mate combined with the traces of wine, risotto, and lemon.

Delicious.

Then Krispin lifted his head and grinned through kiss-swollen lips at him. "And this."

Krispin slid his hand down Wash's back and gripped his ass. Rocking his hips, he pressed their groins together. His vampire's hard erection slotted up beside Wash's own, and a low moan rocketed past his lips.

"W-We should head to your apartment," Wash muttered.

"Oh?" Krispin arched a brow. "I have an office nearby. No one will bother us there."

Wash gave his vampire a toothy grin. "But I can't wash that lady's shitty perfume off you in your office."

Krispin tipped his head back and laughed, his blue eyes twinkling. "True." Stepping backward, he squeezed Wash's hand. "Let's go."

Then Wash's vampire led the way.

Wash had hated leaving Krispin's side to continue his search. It had been necessary, however. He had to locate where Chasis was roosting.

It would have been easier if Krispin hadn't asked for him to take along one of his enforcers.

When Wash had pointed out that a vampire enforcer couldn't fly, Krispin had growled low in his throat and asked what that had to do with anything.

Wash had hated explaining that most of the places he would be exploring were on roofs, in nearby treetops, or even a few caves. Chasis had been circling the area for days, and being in the city with traffic, his scent had been spread far and wide. He had to find him fast, before he healed well enough to make another play at Dloben.

Krispin had been more worried about Chasis attacking Wash again. Then he'd asked him to wait for back-up from Chieftain Kinsey. When Wash had refused, he requested to be called as soon as Wash had located him. He'd told him he could get vampires to any part of his territory far faster than waiting on Chieftain Kinsey's men.

Once again, Wash had needed to explain that if vampires showed up, there was no way to keep him from just flying away again.

As much as Wash hated the rift it created between them, he had still left. He felt grateful his mate had set him up with a credit card and clothes that he could shift in without destroying. Well, he had to take the coat off to grow his wings, but that was fine.

Swooping along an air current high in the sky, Wash caught the trail he wanted. The sensitive receptors on his tongue recognized Chasis's scent. He paused there, wings flapping, as he ascertained the swirl of the air currents.

Wash made a decision and carefully started on his way. The sun was due to rise soon, so he would need to find a place to land and don his human skin. He had to admit, being mated definitely gave him an advantage. While Wash couldn't fly around in daylight, he could track from the ground, and Chasis couldn't go anywhere.

Landing near the edge of a forest, Wash eased between trees. He kept careful track of air currents, making certain he stayed downwind of the area he wanted to explore. The first rays of dawn were just beginning to brighten the sky as he spotted a tree stand.

Chasis crouched upon it . . . and he was staring right at Wash.

The gray-hided gargoyle grinned broadly at him. "You

know, Wash, you're not very good at hiding from your query." He scoffed. "No wonder Chieftain Grecian never promoted you."

As Chasis jumped from the tree and began stalking toward him between trees, Wash recalled their prior chieftain. The male had been a tyrant and an asshole. Wash had never tried to get promoted.

Wash also began backing slowly, doing his best to keep plenty of space between them. "Chieftain Grecian was an asshole," he stated belligerently.

"I'm gonna kill you this time, Wash," Chasis claimed, moving closer still. "You haven't called in my location, since I spotted you first."

While what Chasis said was true, Wash pointed at the sky. "Sunrise. You don't have enough time to kill me."

"I'll just do it at sunset tonight," Chasis told him with a nasty, toothy grin. "You really should have planned ahead."

"I did plan ahead," Wash countered.

Then the sun peeked over the horizon, and Chasis crouched. He grinned widely as he wrapped his wings around his shoulders. "Tomorrow," he said on a cackle.

Wash shook his head as his query turned to stone, and he took on his human form. He pulled his phone out of his pocket and called his chieftain.

"Good morning, Wash," Chieftain Kinsey greeted. "How are you and your mate today?"

"Good morning, Chieftain," Wash replied, staring at Chasis's stone form. "I'm well, and as far as I know, Krispin is fine, too."

"Not with him, then?"

"No, Chieftain."

Chieftain Kinsey sighed. "I had hoped you would change your mind, and you were calling to tell me to send another tracker. Bonding with your mate is important, Wash."

Wash felt his face flush a little as he cleared his throat. "We did bond, Chieftain. I'm in my human form right now."

"Oh!" The sound of the chieftain shifting around came through the line. "Your sunrise must be a smidge before ours. It's still dark out here."

With the clutch located a couple of hours to the southwest, Wash hadn't even considered that possibility. "Huh." He rested his hand on his hip before quickly continuing, "I'm standing in front of Chasis's stone form. Can you have enforcers at these coordinates before sunset?" Lowering his phone, Wash quickly typed out a text message.

"Hold on."

Chieftain Kinsey fell silent for several minutes, so Wash figured he was checking.

After five minutes, Chieftain Kinsey stated, "Maybe, but it'll be tight."

"Then may I respectfully request bringing my mate's enforcers in on this? They are only a couple of hours drive on back roads."

Wash held his breath, wondering what his chieftain would say.

CHAPTER SEVEN

K rispin glanced at his watch.
Ten minutes to sunset.

Peering amidst the trees, Krispin confirmed that everything and everyone was in place. His vampires were spread around Chasis's statue, each holding the ends of a rope like spokes on a wheel. The only things missing were the gargoyle enforcers.

According to his last report, they were twenty minutes out. *Good thing Wash convinced Chieftain Kinsey to let us help.*

Krispin tightened his arm around Wash, inordinately pleased his beloved had offered such loyalty.

"And you're certain he won't be able to tear through that with his claws?"

Focusing on Wash, Krispin saw his beloved point at the thick net draped around the stone gargoyle. With the heavy weights around it, the circular bindings reminded him of a fishing net. The ropes his vampires held were attached to those weights, and upon pulling, the net would tighten.

Nodding, Krispin gave Wash an encouraging smile. "A vampire's talons can't slice through those cables, so I highly doubt a gargoyle's claws can." Then he pointed and winked. "Of course, you're welcome to try before he wakes up."

For an instant, Krispin thought Wash would take him up on his offer. Then his beloved relaxed against him again and shook his head.

"I trust you."

A burst of pleasure coursed through him at those simple

words. "Thank you," he murmured before pressing a kiss to Wash's temple.

Wash smiled at him, wrapping a wing around them both. *Gods, that's sexy.*

Krispin loved his beloved's wings.

"Sunset," Wash whispered.

Amidst the trees, it was nearly full dark. Krispin figured Wash knew the exact moment of sunrise and sunset due to his gargoyle heritage. Just because he was no longer ruled by it probably didn't change that.

An angry bellow erupted from the gargoyle before them. Chasis lunged off the ground. He attempted to spread his wings as he swung his arms, slicing at the heavy cable. While his claws left shallow grooves in the net, it held.

When that didn't work, Chasis twisted and yanked, attempting to pull the lines out of Enforcer Carmine's hands.

Krispin would guess that he chose her because she was female. It didn't work. She easily held her own, using a tree as leverage.

Smarter not harder, Krispin thought with a smirk.

"What's the meaning of this, vampires?" Chasis roared, peering around the group. Then his gaze landed on Wash, and hatred sparked in his eyes. "You! This is your doing. Release me at once!"

"Actually, it's *your* doing," Wash countered, crossing his arms over his chest. "You're the moron who refused to obey your chieftain's orders and went rogue."

"I obey my chieftain," Chasis countered. "When Chieftain Grecian returns, he will honor me for retaining our ways."

Krispin rolled his eyes before focusing on Wash. "Is he really that thick?"

"I guess so," Wash replied with a shrug. He scowled at Chasis as he stated, "Chieftain Grecian was bested by Kinsey. He was taken by an elder. He's not returning to the Aerasceatle clutch."

"Regardless. Vampires have no say in gargoyle law," Chasis spouted. "These people can't capture me. Release me right this fucking minute, or I'll lodge a complaint to the elders."

"Huh." Krispin couldn't stop his chuckle as he squeezed Wash's opposite hip. "He really is that dense. How about that." Then he smirked at Chasis. "I am Master Krispin Stearling. You are in my territory without announcing your presence. Per paranormal culture, I can detain you in order to verify your intentions here. So, tell me who you are and what you're doing here, gargoyle."

Chasis curled his lip, showing off plenty of pointed teeth. "As if you don't already know I'm Chasis of Clutch Aerasceatle. And I'm here to find the deserter, Dloben, and return him to his place at the clutch for when Chieftain Grecian returns."

"Why are you under the impression that Chieftain Grecian will be returning to that clutch?" Krispin couldn't help but ask. "We were notified a new chieftain led."

Narrowing his eyes, Chasis shook his head. "I have a contact who works for one of the elders. He assures me that Chieftain Grecian will be cleared and returned to the clutch."

"Who is your contact?" Krispin asked, barely restraining curling his lip upon hearing the distasteful news.

Is there truly a few rotten apples amidst the gargoyle Circle of Elders?

Krispin knew it wouldn't be the first time power corrupted.

Chasis scoffed. "I'll not reveal my source until after I'm released."

Damn. Not that dumb then.

"Very well, Chasis. Per the request of Chieftain Kinsey, I have been authorized to secure you and transfer you to—"

"No!" Chasis screeched. "I am well within my rights—"

Krispin held up his hand as he interrupted him in turn. "Unless you can tell me someone who will substantiate your claims, my hands are tied," he claimed, staring at Chasis intently. "The missives I have received are different than yours. I would need to verify the change."

He could practically see the wheels turning in Chasis's head. Due to the indignation and anger rolling off the gargoyle, he couldn't confirm whether or not Chasis believed his words.

Did he really have a contact? Was someone working under the elders really trying to undo all Chieftain Kinsey's changes?

Then another thought hit Krispin.

Wash?

Krispin felt Wash tense beside him before sneaking a quick look his way.

Yeah. It's me. A bonded vampire forms a mental link with their partner. I completely forgot about it. Try saying something back to me.

When several heartbeats went by and Krispin still hadn't heard Wash in his mind, he tried again.

Think of yourself talking on the phone to me, except just in your head.

A second later, Krispin fought back a smile.

Krispin?

That's the way. "Please note, Chasis," Krispin stated out loud. "I can't help you if you don't help me first."

Your sense of smell is better than a vampires'. All I scent is rage. As annoying as it was to accept, Krispin knew it was true. *Can you tell if Chasis believes his words?*

Yeah. He believes them. He seriously thinks he's getting orders from someone connected to the elders. Shit!

Krispin silently thought the same thing. Done waiting, he turned his attention to Ridger, who handled one of the ropes. "Second Ridger, please secure the rogue." Upon seeing Chasis's feral glare, he shrugged. "Sorry, Chasis. I gave you a chance."

"You'll be sorry," Chasis vowed. "You'll *all* be sorry."

"Of course, we will," Krispin replied blithely, tired of the male's bluster. "Wash, will you check to see how far out our friends are?"

Wash pulled out his phone and shot off a text.

A chime drifted through the trees, drawing Krispin's attention behind him. He turned in time to see Chieftain Kinsey appear through the foliage. There were a couple of other gargoyles with him that Krispin didn't recognize.

In truth, the only reason Krispin knew the chieftain on sight was because Wash had video chatted with him while Krispin had been in the room.

"Welcome to my territory, Chieftain Kinsey," Krispin said by way of greeting, holding out his hand. "It's a pleasure to finally meet you in person."

"And you as well, Master Krispin," Chieftain Kinsey replied, taking his hand. After releasing the handshake, the large, yellowish-orange gargoyle pulled Wash into a brief hug. "Congratulations, Washington. We will be sorry to see you go."

"Thank you, Chieftain," Wash replied as the chieftain released him. Just as he turned toward a red-hided gargoyle, a big grin on his face, Chasis interrupted.

"What the hell are you congratulating him for?" Chasis sneered. "He's a useless tracker. Always letting his query know where he is. Shoulda killed him on the roof."

"You got a mouthy one on your hands, Chieftain Kinsey," Krispin commented with a shake of his head. "And he's claiming that someone working under one of the elders is trying to reinstate Grecian."

"I'll have to question him on that one," Chieftain Kinsey replied on a growl. "Thank you for the warning. I'll contact Elder Vermidian. He's the one who oversaw my challenge."

Then the chieftain grinned coldly at Chasis. "And I was congratulating Wash because he found his mate. Didn't you wonder how all the vampires knew right where you were?"

Chasis's expression suddenly turned stricken . . . and he shut up.

Finally.

Wash touched Krispin's arm. "Mate, I'd like you to meet Lionad, my younger brother."

Krispin turned toward the tall, slender, red gargoyle Wash had been heading toward a moment ago. He smiled as he watched the pair exchange a hug. Lionad offered his brother congratulations, although his expression appeared sad.

"We will miss you," Lionad claimed.

"The brother of my beloved is welcome to visit my territory anytime," Krispin told him, holding out his hand. "Good to meet you."

"Thank you." Lionad shook and released. "Simon, too?"

Krispin lifted a brow at Wash.

His human mate.

Upon hearing his beloved's voice in his mind, Krispin grinned at Lionad. "Simon, too."

"I bet Simon would love to hike some of these trails," Lionad commented, peering around the dark forest. "He loves nature."

"Chieftain Kinsey?" Basques called, having passed off his rope to a different gargoyle.

"Yes, Enforcer Basques?" Chieftain Kinsey didn't appear surprised to see Krispin's enforcer approach him.

"I'd like to demand restitution for the pain Chasis has inflicted on my beloved."

"Come to think of it, so would I," Krispin commented with a smirk. Upon seeing his enforcer's scowl, he lifted his hand, palm out. "But I waive my right, since his attack on Wash brought him to me."

Chieftain Kinsey nodded. "Enforcer Basques, I

acknowledge and uphold your right for restitution."

"What!" Chasis cried.

Evidently, that had brought him out of his brooding stupor.

Without bothering to turn to address Chasis or his outburst, Chieftain Kinsey remained focused on Basques. "Because Chasis has information I need to extract from him, I cannot allow your restitution to be death. However, I understand he had a high position under Grecian, so he had access to some fine things." His smile turned wry as he continued. "I know material goods can't always equate a pound of flesh, but please consider it."

Enforcer Basques nodded once. "I understand, Chieftain. I accept, although I wish for Dloben to be present with me when we decide on what *fine things* he could want." Clearing his throat, he rubbed the back of his neck. "I don't want to accidentally take something of Chasis's that has negative connotations for him."

"Of course," Chieftain Kinsey replied with a dip of his chin. "I look forward to hearing when you and Dloben decide to visit."

"Thank you."

Over the next couple of hours, Chasis was secured and transported to an underground holding area beneath the vampires' hotel. Those gargoyles who wished were given rooms for the next two nights, giving them time to explore the city. All the ones Chieftain Kinsey had brought were mated, so it was safe.

The chieftain's mate, Jimmy, as well as Simon, had been waiting in one of the gargoyles' SUVs. A couple of gargoyles chose to return home immediately, since they're mates were not there. Another pair that had joined Chieftain Kinsey had actually been mates—Enforcer Biers and his lion shifter mate,

Dyson.

That evening, Krispin and his inner circle — mates in tow — sat in his office with Chieftain Kinsey, Enforcer Biers, Lionad, and their mates. They enjoyed a low-key dinner delivered to the room as well as wine and spirits. Krispin found he enjoyed the chieftain's laid-back approach to discussing topics that impacted both their peoples. The gargoyle didn't stand on ceremony.

"So, you've been eating your cinnamon every day?"

Krispin cocked his head, his brows furrowing. Meeting the chieftain's gaze, he tried to understand the question. He couldn't.

"Sorry. Cinnamon?" Krispin glanced around the group, realizing everyone else had just shut up and were staring at him. "What?"

"You didn't tell him?" Chieftain Kinsey sounded incredulous as he focused on Wash.

"Oh, shit." Wash shifted in his seat as he stared at Krispin with wide eyes. "Oh. Oh, I thought you knew . . . because of — " He waved toward Basques and Dloben.

Krispin felt his gut roll as the realization hit. "I'm missing something rather important, aren't I?"

Basques groaned long and low. "Aaaaah, man!" He scowled at Wash. "Just because I bonded with a gargoyle didn't mean I told him everything."

"What's going on?" Ridger glanced around the group, his body tensing.

Lifting his hands, Krispin called, "Everyone, relax." Then he reached over and took Wash's free hand. He didn't like the way his beloved's other hand trembled just a little before he rested the tumbler he held on the arm of his chair to hide it. "Beloved, whatever it is, we'll work through it together."

Wash took a deep fortifying breath, then let it out slowly. "Okay." Staring beseechingly at Krispin, he asked, "You're aware that all gargoyles are male, and we have the ability to make our male mates pregnant?"

Krispin sucked in a swift breath. "Oh, I do recall talking about that," he murmured. In fact, it was one of the reasons he'd ended up dispatching one ex-enforcer of his. She'd been prejudiced and had attempted to attack Dloben. "Okay, yes. And we didn't use condoms when you fucked me." His stomach twisted, and the fantastic finger foods threatened to make a reappearance. "You think I could be pregnant?"

Yep, bile in the back of my throat.

He swallowed convulsively, then lifted his whiskey to his lips, only to pause.

Right. Alcohol.

Leaning forward, Krispin set the tumbler on the expansive coffee table, his vision beginning to swim.

Damn.

"Here. Here."

To Krispin's surprise, Jimmy was pressing a water bottle into his palm.

"Take a drink. Breathe slow and deep."

Krispin did as the small human suggested. After downing a mouthful, he took a second one. "Thank you, Jimmy," he murmured, his head beginning to settle.

"And the guys asked if you ate anything with cinnamon in it because it's a natural contraceptive," Jimmy told him, still standing nearby. He began ticking things off on his fingers. "Cinnamon rolls. Cinnamon toast. Cinnamon in your coffee. French toast with cinnamon and sugar. Cinnamon *Life* cereal. Cinnamon on your crème brulee."

Racking his brain, Krispin tried to think of anything he would have eaten in the last couple of days that had cinnamon in it. He drew a blank. Whether food or drink, he was coming up with a big fat zero.

"Not that I can recall," Krispin admitted.

"What about you, Wash?" Chieftain Kinsey asked, snagging Jimmy's hand and drawing him back to his side.

Wash sighed deeply. Meeting Krispin's eyes, he wore a pensive expression. "I can't think of a damn thing, either."

"Well." Krispin clicked his tongue as the ramifications surged through him. "That would be . . . an interesting development."

CHAPTER EIGHT

Interesting development?

That was the understatement of the century.

"Holy fuck," Wash whispered. "A hatchling."

Lionad chuckled and hefted his rum glass. "Way to go, bro."

Simon snickered.

"Wait, wait," Ridger called out, lifting both hands, one holding his own whiskey tumbler. "There's no guarantee anyone is pregnant, right?" He focused on Krispin. "'Cause he's a gargoyle, Kris, you have to bottom to finish the bond, so Wash can go through molt, but after that?"

Krispin cleared his throat, frowning at his friend. "Are you asking about my sex practices with my beloved?"

Ridger's eyes widened. "Oh, shit! You did!" He glanced between them as his cheeks and neck took on a scarlet hue. Shifting in his seat, Ridger swallowed so hard his Adam's apple bobbed. "Never been on the receiving end. Guess it wouldn't occur to me that you'd, uh—" Maybe to shut himself up, Ridger took a gulp of his drink.

Shrugging, Krispin murmured, "The things my beloved can do with his tail should be illegal."

Wash felt heat rise on his own skin and hoped his brown hide hid it. He knew Krispin was referring to their time in the shower just over twenty-four hours before . . . and when they'd been in the bathtub together before having to place the net on Chasis. His vampire master had turned into a fiery switch-hitter, and Wash had taken complete advantage.

"How long until we know?" Krispin asked, rubbing his forehead.

"I'm sorry," Wash muttered again.

Krispin shook his head as he squeezed Wash's hand. "Not your fault, my beloved." His tone took on a soothing quality as he leaned toward him. "I was aware that you could impregnate male mates, so it was my responsibility, too. We had a miscommunication, and if I end up carrying your egg, so be it." Chuckling huskily, Krispin told him, "While I'd never given the idea of *me* carrying the child much thought, I've always enjoyed kids."

Relief flooded Wash. His mate was taking it so well. He knew he had to do the same.

Wash sighed, then leaned toward Krispin and pressed a light peck to his lips. "Thanks, Kris. I admit I looked forward to someday having hatchlings." With a shrug of his shoulder, he gave his vampire a wry smile. "I just figured I'd have more time to get to know my mate first."

Krispin nodded, winked, then swept his gaze around the group again. "So? How long until we know?" he asked again.

When everyone just started looking around at each other, Wash frowned. "Really? No one?" Wash pressed.

Chieftain Kinsey frowned. "When was the last time a hatchling was born into the Aerasceatle clutch?" he pointed out. "None of us were having children because those mated didn't want to raise a child in that hate-filled environment, and those who created the environment were all unmated." Then a glower darkened his expression. "Except my father."

"Your father!" Jimmy sounded excited.

Confusion in his scent, Chieftain Kinsey picked up his human and set him on his lap. "I wouldn't even know who to call to try to talk to my father, not that I'd want to anyway."

Snuggling on Chieftain Kinsey's lap, Jimmy snickered. "But we talk to your mom every week, and she had three hatchlings. Call her."

"My brilliant mate," Chieftain Kinsey purred. After pecking Jimmy's lips, he pulled out his phone.

Wash knew they spoke of a strong-willed human named Wendy. She'd been bonded with the gargoyle, Creasis, who'd ended up adopting Grecian's views and had turned into a bigoted asshole. When Creasis had begun terrorizing their middle child, Wendy had helped Conchlin find a new, better clutch and escape his terror.

Over the century that had followed, Wendy had continued to help as she could, even though she was the mate of one of the inner circle. The changes in her mate had strained their bond. Eventually, the impact to the gargoyle had weakened him, allowing Kinsey to best him in a fight. He'd been one of those taken by the gargoyle elder after the leadership change.

Wendy had chosen to live with Conchlin and was welcomed by the Falias clutch in Colorado. As far as Wash knew, she was still vibrant and healthy. The same probably couldn't be said for Creasis, regardless of where he'd ended up.

"Kinsey, honey! How are you?" Wendy's joyful voice came through the line, and every paranormal in the room had no trouble hearing her. "Is Jimmy with you?"

"Hi, Mom," Chieftain Kinsey replied. "Yeah. He's here. Let me put you on speaker."

A heartbeat later, Wendy's voice came through the speakerphone. "Hi, Jimmy! You there?"

"Here," Jimmy replied.

"Are you keeping my little boy in line?"

A few chuckles sounded through the room. While Kinsey was the chieftain of the clutch, he was Wendy's youngest. That meant he would always be her little boy.

Jimmy laughed, clearly delighted by his mother-in-law. "Always doing my best."

"Good, good." Wendy hummed. "From the sounds of it

over there, ya'll aren't alone."

"We're not, Mom," Chieftain Kinsey confirmed. "We're actually being entertained by Master Krispin Stearling. We're in his territory at the moment." He leaned forward and placed the phone on the middle coffee table. "He's a vampire, and he mated with Washington."

Wendy squealed—actually *squealed*. "How exciting!" she cried. "Washington was always such a fine young man." Then she raised her voice and called, "Congratulations!"

Wash felt his skin heat again, even as he leaned forward, too. "Thank you, Mrs. Wendy. I am truly blessed."

Maybe even more than I first realized.

"Pssshht," Wendy sounded through the line. "It's just Wendy. So, let's hear Krispin's voice. You there, hon? You gonna take good care of our Washington?"

With an amused smile on his face, Krispin called, "I'll do the best I can, Wendy. Thank you for the congratulations. I know this is a little unorthodox, but I'm hoping you can provide me with some information."

"Of course! Need some embarrassing Wash stories from when he was a hatchling?" Wendy giggled. "A lady never tells her age, but between you and me, I was around then."

While Wash felt his face flame, Krispin chuckled deeply. "Oh, so very tempting, Wendy." Before she could go off on another tangent, he quickly added, "However, we've run into a bit of a question that none of the guys here seem to know how to answer."

Krispin glanced around, then grimaced, probably realizing he had to start talking about his sex life.

"Of course, hon." Wendy seemed to call everyone that. "I've seen plenty along the way. What can I help with?"

"Well, Wash and I had a little bit of a miscommunication about the whole cinnamon thing."

Wendy gasped through the line. "You all *forgot*?"

Clearing his throat once more, Krispin winced. "Something

like that. How long after, uh . . . intercourse . . . would one know if the male is pregnant?" By the time he finished speaking, his cheeks were scarlet.

Not a bad look on the vampire, if the rosy cheeks were caused by something other than embarrassment.

Trying to be supportive, Wash squeezed Krispin's hand.

Wendy remained quiet for a long few seconds. "Oh my gods," she finally stated. "You forgot to tell him about cinnamon, Wash?"

A snicker-snort noise came through the line, along with some gasping.

Wash exchanged looks with the other men. Lionad was smirking at him. Simon had his hand over his mouth, but it was obvious that he was giggling.

The others all sported various expressions of amusement and sympathy.

Sighing, Wash realized he was going to have to bite the bullet. "Yes. He has another mated gargoyle in his clutch, so it didn't occur to me that he didn't know, and I . . . gods." He huffed a sigh. "Yes, I completely screwed up." Wash cast an apologetic look in Krispin's direction, who smiled, then asked, "So do you know?"

"Of course, I do, hon," Wendy immediately replied, although mirth remained in her tone. "It might have been a few centuries, but I had three of them, you know."

"So?" Krispin pressed, appearing to get a little antsy.

Since Krispin was a vampire master, Wash doubted the man had much trouble getting swift and concise answers. The scent of annoyance had begun to emanate from his mate. Wash massaged the hand he held, hoping to soothe him.

"Paranormals are always faster," Wendy explained. "Pee on a stick in a week, and you'll know. And before you ask" — she continued swiftly — "yes, human pregnancy tests work. Just be sure to get one of the higher-end ones."

Before Wash could begin his *thank yous* — *Three days. Damn. I've really known my mate less than a week* — Wendy began speaking again.

"Now, remember. Someone impregnated by a gargoyle is pregnant on average for three months. The egg will grow to about five inches in diameter before it's ready to be laid." She huffed a sigh. "And, yes, for men, it's through your rectum. Work on stretching when you're coming to be due."

Wendy said it so matter-of-factly, it took a few heartbeats for Wash to process her advice.

Stretching.

Oh gods. Shoot me now.

"You're never knocking me up, handsome," Simon whispered, although everyone in the room heard it.

Lionad leveled a heated smile on his human. "Never say never, baby."

She was still talking.

"The standard birthing time is anywhere from four to eight hours, so try not to fret." Humming, Wendy added, "Oh, have an incubator on hand. The egg needs to be kept sanitary for another three months as it grows. The egg starts with a leathery hide, which allows it to expand. Then about a month before hatching, it firms up and becomes brittle. When the baby is ready . . . *crack*." She chuckled, then sighed. "Watching a little one break out of his shell is truly a thing of beauty."

Wash's brain was on complete overload. He blinked, frowned, blinked again. It wasn't until he heard Krispin say, "Thank you, Wendy. We appreciate all the information."

A smacking sound came through the line just as Wendy cried, "Oh, one more thing. The bruise."

The bruise?

"Bruise?" Krispin repeated.

"Yes, yes," Wendy replied, sounding pleased that she'd remembered. "With men, your appendix acts as a womb. So you expand a little sideways and you end up with what appears to be an impressive bruise on your back. And, yes, it does hurt. Sorry." She chuckled, not sounding sorry at all. "It's really an indicator of how soon it'll be to laying time. When the egg is ready, the paleness in the center of the bruise will be about two inches in diameter and you'll be able to feel the curvature of the egg underneath the skin."

"So it's a visible thing?" Krispin sounded concerned.

"Oh, yes, of course," Wendy confirmed. "You'll look like you have a baby bump for sure." As if realizing what a problem that could be, she added, "Of course, for the last month or so you'll want to stay away from unknowledgeable humans."

"Of course," Krispin whispered. Straightening, he rubbed the back of his neck. "That would be . . . ill-timing, but we'd deal with it."

A fresh wave of concern flooding him, Wash squeezed his hand again. "What do you mean?"

Ridger answered. "You remember that uncomfortable lunch we had to muddle through?" As Wash began to nod, "Well, the park is already half-finished, and it should be completed within two and a half months. There's a grand opening gala." Ridger pointed at Krispin. "And being the bequeather of the grant, Krispin is expected to be there."

"Oh." Wash whispered that one word on a sigh.

"If it comes to that, we'll figure it out, my beloved," Krispin encouraged, lifting his hand to kiss his palm. "Besides. We don't even know if it's an issue at this point. No sense in borrowing trouble. Right?"

"Right."

As they'd had their side conversation, Wendy had been chatting with her son. Suddenly, her question cut through the conversation. "So, Kinsey. When are you going to make me a grandma?"

Chieftain Kinsey's eyes widened, looking for all the world like a deer caught in the headlights. Jimmy wasn't much better. He was staring at Kinsey with his mouth opening and closing as no sound came out.

After several heartbeats where no one said a word, Wendy harrumphed. "Oh, I know the line didn't drop. Answer the question, son."

Tipping back his head, gritting his teeth, Chieftain Kinsey appeared for all the world as a man in pain. "Well," he began slowly. "We're still getting the clutch sorted, and I would really like to have a stable environment to bring your grandson into the world." Holding Jimmy's gaze, Kinsey added, "Plus, my mate is pretty damn young. Only twenty-three. We haven't talked about hatchlings, yet."

"Oh, pish-posh," Wendy replied flippantly. "Twenty-three is plenty old enough, and you've been working out the kinks in that clutch for over a year. With Creasis dead, I'm starting to gray. I want grandchildren before I'm too old to play with them."

Chieftain Kinsey's jaw sagged open. "F-Father is dead?"

That was obviously news.

"Of course, dear. What did you think was going to happen to him?"

"Well, I guess, um." Chieftain Kinsey grimaced as Jimmy rubbed his hand up and down his chest. "I guess I didn't really think about it." Then he cleared his throat and asked, "How do you know?"

Wendy sighed deeply, her tone losing its joviality. "Well, baby, I felt the bond snap. It was painful. I won't lie to you. But"—she sighed again—"our bond had been stretched so thin for so long. It didn't come as a surprise."

"That's why you moved to Conchlin's clutch," Chieftain Kinsey mused, nuzzling Jimmy's neck, probably for comfort. "Did it happen before or after your move?"

"After," Wendy told him. "But I knew it was coming. As his mate, Elder Vermidian sent me a message."

"Why didn't you say anything to me?"

There was no mistaking the pain in Chieftain Kinsey's voice.

"Oh, honey," Wendy murmured. "What good would that have done? I expect I'll have another few decades. And I've had centuries." Then her voice perked up. "Which is why I'm so happy both my boys are mated. Double the chance to be a grandma!"

"Like a dog with a bone." Jimmy mumbled the words, but everyone heard it.

Even Wendy laughed. "Yes, sweet, Jimmy." Then she sobered. "You listen here, sweetie. Hatchlings are a blessing. Even if they don't turn out the way you want them to."

Wash knew that Wendy referred to her eldest son, Fastian, who had been taken away by an elder for attacking his brother's mate after he'd lost a challenge.

At least two of her three children had turned out fantastic.

"I actually have one more question," Basques commented, leaning forward.

"And who are you, dear?"

Basques smiled. "I'm Enforcer Basques Grouper. I'm a vampire bonded with Dloben, from your old clutch."

Wendy gasped. "Dloben found his mate? Congrats to you both!" Her enthusiasm had returned.

"Thank you," Dloben called shyly.

"You're welcome. What's your question, dear?"

Staring into his glass, Basques asked, "Can vampires have whiskey when they're pregnant?"

Dloben's eyes widened, a questioning look on his face. Basques quickly shook his head and jerked his chin in Krispin's direction.

Wash followed his look and spotted the look of longing on

Krispin's face as he gazed at his discarded whiskey tumbler.

Wendy's laughter came through the line. "Of course, dear! Alcohol burns up differently in a paranormal. Or even a human bonded with one. Totally safe."

"Oh, thank fuck," Krispin muttered.

Krispin leaned forward, grabbed his glass, then gulped the remainder of the amber liquid.

CHAPTER NINE

Staring down at the piss test, Krispin breathed deeply. *Just pee on the stick and it's done.*

Krispin still couldn't figure out how he'd ended up here.

Oh, right. Yes, I can. I charged into bonding with my mate like a bull in a china shop.

Rolling his eyes, Krispin couldn't remember the last time he'd pushed so hard for something to happen. He really should have thought everything through. Unfortunately, mating hormones developed damn fast.

After letting out another sigh, Krispin aimed before mentally encouraging his bladder to let go. For a second, he wasn't certain if he'd actually be able to release a drop. Then his groin relaxed, and his stream coursed out of him.

Hitting his thumb, Krispin winced as he adjusted.

Ugh.

Krispin doused the soft end, then carefully set it on several wads of toilet paper. After he finished peeing, he shook off. He washed up before tucking away however, scrubbing his hands briskly.

Then Krispin closed the lid on the toilet, sat on it, and waited. He could hear Wash pacing in their bedroom beyond. The gargoyle had offered to sit in there with him, but Krispin honestly didn't think he would have been able to take the test in front of him.

While Krispin had never been a prude about peeing while turned away from another person—male or female—it had taken damn near everything in him to get his bladder to unclench while by himself.

Krispin rested his forearms on his thighs and hung his head. He'd been doing everything he could to remain strong, confident, calm, in front of his beloved. Below the surface, he knew turbulent fear and uncertainty ruled.

Pregnant?

A gargoyle egg?

Could a gargoyle be an heir to a vampire coven?

Would a babe between them have combined similarities or take after one or another dominant gene?

Which gene was actually dominant?

At that thought, Krispin straightened and sat back on the porcelain throne. That, at least, he could answer. Whatever breed paranormal had the longest lifespan, that was the dominant one. That meant the gargoyle gene.

Over the long years Krispin had led, he'd heard of many different types of paranormals bonding.

A shifter and a human always produced a shifter.

A shifter and a witch or warlock created a magick wielder with increased senses but couldn't shift.

A witch or warlock and a vampire created a hybrid that needed blood sparingly while being able to do magick.

A gargoyle who bonded with a male fated mate always beget another gargoyle. Gargoyles who bonded with a female fated mate could possibly create a female with enhanced senses and abilities.

Oh, and demons and angels didn't breed. They were sterile.

Probably because they were created by the gods and not born.

As Krispin thought about all the things he'd heard over the years, something popped into his mind.

What does a fae and any combination produce?

Krispin had no idea.

Glancing at the clock on his phone, Krispin realized he'd

wasted enough time. He swallowed hard and focused to the left. He stared at the pregnancy test.

What did two lines mean again?

He had to double-check the paperwork.

Pregnant.

Oh, holy fuck, I'm really pregnant.

Krispin bit back the whimper that threatened to escape his throat. His pulse rate sped up. He breathed deeply as he tucked his head between his knees.

Upon hearing a soft tapping at the bathroom door, Krispin inhaled slowly and pulled himself together. He straightened. "Coming," he called. After rubbing his palms over his face one more time, Krispin knew he couldn't stall any more.

Turning, Krispin headed out to tell his beloved the news.

Krispin opened the door and peered into Wash's honey-brown eyes. He saw the questions there. Peeling his tongue from the roof of his mouth, he forced moisture into his throat.

"Beloved, we are pregnant."

For a second, Wash just stared at him. Then his eyes widened. Finally, he barked a harsh cry, and he stumbled backward.

Growing worried about that response, Krispin didn't know whether to head after him or back up a step. He hated the uncertainty . . . the hesitation.

Then Wash lunged for Krispin and wrapped him in strong brown arms and large black wings. He clutched him close. Tucking his face into Krispin's neck, he trilled as he clung to him.

Krispin felt the soothing vibration, and a calm washed over him. As he sank into his beloved's embrace, he clutched his lover close. After a few seconds of trilling and nuzzling, Krispin realized what had set his gargoyle off.

The scent of his own nerves, which must have flooded the bathroom during his wait, would have hit Wash like a fist to the face.

"I'm okay," Krispin assured, finding his tongue. He ran his hands up and down Wash's back. "We'll both be okay." Scraping his fangs along his beloved's neck tendons, he strove to get his attention. "You and me, my beloved. We'll be the best damn parents on the planet."

"You don't hate me?" Wash rumbled, finally ceasing his trilling and lifting his head just enough to meet his gaze. "I promise I didn't do it on purpose."

Krispin felt his heart break. "Oh, my sweet beloved." He lifted a hand and threaded it into Wash's hair. "I never thought you did it on purpose. Not for one second." Chuckling softly, Krispin shrugged. "We just got carried away like teenagers. It happens." After a wink, he added, "Even to hundreds plus year old paranormals. You *are* pretty special, after all."

"You are, too." Wash pressed his lips to Krispin's in a hard, bruising kiss for one heartbeat, two. "You, too."

Chuckling huskily, Krispin waggled his brows. "So, first things first, congratulations sex."

To Krispin's amusement and delight, he felt Wash's hands lift his ass, so he wrapped his legs around his beloved. He loved having a lover as powerful as himself, and he couldn't deny that it did things for him—pushed buttons he hadn't even known he possessed.

Gods, Fate is good.

As Krispin felt Wash carry him toward the bed, Wash asked, "And after that?" He laid him down on the bed.

"After that." Krispin began helping his lover divest them of all clothes. "We'll go out, drink a glass of champagne, and share our good news with the coven."

"It's a deal."

Krispin gave as good as he got as he tussled with his lover in bed, rolling, kissing, sucking, and nipping, loving every second of it.

Almost three months later

"No, I'm sorry, Mayor Bickerman." Krispin rolled his eyes as he ground his teeth together. "Tiffany, of course. No, I'm sorry, Tiffany. My receptionist told you right. I can't make the meeting at City Hall this afternoon."

Or any meetings for the next week or two.

Krispin shifted in his seat, trying to find a comfortable position. At eleven weeks pregnant—*still feels weird to think that*—with another week or so to go, he was damn uncomfortable almost all the time. Only lying on his left side with his right leg raised and forward on a pillow allowed his body to release enough tension for him to sleep at night.

"Krispin, you know you're an integral part of this," Tiffany pressed. "Your insight is needed."

Sigh. Sleep. A nap sounds damn good right about now.

"I apologize, Tiffany, but it can't be helped. My partners know all our parameters."

"It's not the same," Tiffany countered. "Our investors need to see the grant holder front and center."

"I'm afraid I'm injured." Krispin had to tell the damn stupid pushy mayor something. "Nothing life-threatening. It just prohibits my maneuverability."

"What?" Tiffany shrieked. "That's terrible! Is it bad? I'll bring over lunch, and we'll conference it."

Krispin rolled his eyes. "No, you don't have to come here. I—" Hearing the dial tone, he gritted his teeth.

"Oh gods, now what do I do?" Krispin glanced at the time. He had exactly thirty-seven minutes to come up with a plan. Punching a number on his phone, he dialed the infirmary. "Doctor Ward? Come to my office at once, and bring ideas on how to hide my condition from the mayor with you."

"Be right there, Master," Doctor Ward promised.

They'd been preparing for this for weeks, after all. They'd known they would only be able to put the mayor off for so long.

Hopefully, he'll have come up with something.

Krispin hit another number.

"Oh, gods. Bet that call with the mayor didn't go very well."

Smirking upon hearing the annoyance in his beloved's tone, Krispin replied, "Of course, it didn't. Will you come here and be the doting and worried fiancé?"

Letting out a snarl, Wash grumbled, "I *am* the doting and worried fiancé."

After Krispin had finished chuckling, he realized his gargoyle had already disconnected the line. Finally, he called Ridger.

"Didn't go well, huh?" his second answered by way of greeting.

"You know her."

Ridger groaned. "Sadly, yes. I'm the one who's had to deal with her for the last couple of weeks while you gave her the run-around," he reminded him. "What do you need?"

"She's headed over here with feel-good food." Krispin scoffed. "No idea what that will entail. I'm about to ring the kitchen, but I wanted to let you and Basques know that we'll be conference calling."

"Oh, goody," Ridger grumbled — not because he didn't enjoy modern technology, but because it would waste everyone's time. "I'll get it set up over here."

"Thank you, my friend."

"Good luck."

Krispin groaned, letting his buddy hear it, who laughed — *bastard* — before he hung up.

Sometimes being the vampire master of a city really sucked. He hated politics. Poking at his phone again, he had one more call to make — the need for comfort, healing food.

Just as Krispin hung up his phone, his door banged open. He spotted Wash striding through first. He was followed by

Doctor Ward. To his surprise, the vampire pushed a wheel-chair full of goodies before him.

"Okay. Quick now." Doctor Ward indicated the chair as he picked everything up and set it aside. "In you get."

While surprised, Krispin didn't question him. He transferred to the chair and settled in.

Immediately, the doc lifted one leg extension of the chair, making his left leg stick out straight. Then he took off his shoe and sock and clasped a cast around that leg, covering it from upper thigh to foot. Next, he held up another couple of items.

"Jacket and button-down off, please, Master," the doc ordered.

Intrigued, Krispin quickly complied, leaning forward awkwardly over his partially immobilized leg. Fortunately, Wash quickly jumped in to help, pulling his clothes from him. It left him in a white undershirt.

"This goes on your left arm," Doctor Ward ordered, holding out another fake cast.

Krispin took it in stride.

Then the doc wrapped a sling around him, holding the casted arm close to his chest.

Finally, Wash returned his jacket to his shoulders, tucking it around him as if to ward off a chill.

After all that, Doctor Ward began draping a large blanket over his lap. It fell in voluminous folds across his legs and waist. "You were in a car accident," he explained with a wink. "Broken leg, cracked ribs, which explains the extra padding around the middle to keep you comfortable." The doc tucked the blanket around his waist. "Plus, a heavily sprained left wrist." He smirked as Wash moved his normal rolling chair to the corner of his office and positioned his wheelchair behind his desk. "Good thing you're right-handed. Right?"

Krispin barked a laugh. "Absolutely."

Doctor Ward grinned. "Now then. You have broken bones.

You're in pain. And have limited mobility." He glanced around and positioned himself in a chair. "I'll be hovering. So will your fiancé." He winked. "We'll keep her out of your space and from discovering your secret."

Relief flooding him, Krispin sighed. "Thank you."

"None needed."

Then the food arrived, so Krispin wouldn't be at the mercy of whatever Tiffany had chosen to bring.

CHAPTER TEN

As soon as Tiffany had been ushered into the office by a vampire enforcer, she came rushing toward Krispin, a food bag flopping over her wrist. She even tried to push past Wash, who was leaning against the corner of his mate's desk.

Wash had been doing his best to make it look like he was checking on Krispin, and she just pushed past him. Hooking an arm around her waist, he forced her back to the other side of the desk. He ignored her sputtering and protests.

"Easy, there, Mayor," Wash rumbled, finally releasing her once she stood next to a guest chair opposite the desk. "Please don't crowd my fiancé right now. He needs some space."

Tiffany's face took on a reddish hue, and she scowled at him. "How dare you touch me?" She placed the food bag on the desk and tried to stare down her nose at him. No easy feat when she was three inches shorter than him, even with Wash in his human form. "I could have you sued for assault."

Wash barked a laugh and rolled his eyes. "Yeah, whatever." Upon hearing her outraged gasp, he shook his head. "Look. Krispin is the polite one. I'm the blunt one. He's injured. Keep back."

Krispin issued a deep sigh from behind Wash. "Please do as Wash says, Tiffany." His voice sounded ragged and tired.

Even knowing it was a façade, Wash's heart still felt a pang of ache for his vampire. Taking a step backward and half pivoting, he glanced over his shoulder at him. "You need anything, babe?" Wash asked gently.

Giving him a wan-looking smile, Krispin murmured, "Just

your presence."

Wash smiled as he pulled Krispin's office chair from the corner. He placed it kitty-corner at the desk, then settled into it.

Krispin indicated the chair Tiffany stood next to. "Please, have a seat, Tiffany. I tried to tell you lunch was unnecessary, but—" He left the *you wouldn't listen* left unsaid. "This is one of my assistants. Carmine. She set up the conference call since you decided to be here instead of there."

Carmine had arrived five minutes before Tiffany and had efficiently set up equipment for the call. There was a flat-screen TV on a rolling trolley and a swiveling arm, as well as a camera attached on top. With the way Carmine had positioned it to the desk's right side, as well as where she was standing nearby, it effectively stopped any way of rounding the desk that way, should Tiffany attempt it.

Smart enforcer.

Tiffany's eyes narrowed, anger glinting in their brown depths. Still, she slowly lowered herself into the indicated chair. After placing her purse on the floor near her feet, she crossed her ankles primly. Then she smoothed imaginary wrinkles out of her skirt and folded her hands in her lap.

Pasting on a perfect politician's smile, Tiffany condescendingly addressed Carmine. "You may start the call."

After glancing Krispin's way and receiving a nod, Carmine obeyed.

Wash had never done anything such as this. His clutch hadn't been up on most of the newer technology, considering Grecian's backward ways. He found himself impressed with the vibrant picture and clear communication.

He also kept his mouth shut and a small smile pasted on his features. The call lasted over an hour, and he found his mind wandering. He wondered what their egg would look like and how badly it would hurt his mate to lay it.

Due to Wendy's warning, Wash had done some research about intense stretching techniques. He wanted that last push to be as painless as possible for Krispin.

The sound of people saying their *thank you*s and *good-bye*s drew Wash back to the present. He blinked, realizing he'd probably missed half the call. Peering at Krispin, he spotted his vampire's amused expression, a knowing gleam in his eyes.

Wash chuckled softly. "Sorry. Not my thing. You know that."

"I know, beloved." Krispin began to reach toward him, but it was his left hand. He faked a hiss and returned his arm to his chest. "Just being here. Remember?"

Reaching out, Wash traced his fingertips up the back of Krispin's neck. "Always."

"So."

Tiffany's harsh voice drew Wash out of the intimate moment.

Damn human.

"I didn't hear about you being in an accident," Tiffany commented. "What happened?"

Wash really didn't like the scents rolling off her . . . smugness, amusement, and satisfaction.

What the hell?

Krispin murmured, "I spent a good bit of money to keep it *out* of the papers. A car accident. Someone T-boned the back end of a town car I was in."

"Whatever injuries did you end up with, darling?" Tiffany asked sweetly.

"Tiffany," Krispin's tone held a clear note of warning. "I'm not your darling. What the hell is your game?" Waving his *good* hand, he commented, "Maybe it's the pain meds, but I'm really not in the mood for politics, so please . . . just spit it out."

Tiffany's smile turned calculating. "I didn't realize vampires could break bones." She tapped her painted lips with one acrylic nail as she mused, "I suppose a car accident could do it. With your increased healing, you should be out of that chair . . . in a week or three? Tough to explain that kind of recovery to the builders. No wonder you sent Ridger to handle the last couple of meetings."

Wash felt his eyes widen before he managed to school his features. Whipping his head around, he took in Krispin's reaction. It wasn't much—just a slight tightening around his lips.

"So you know about us. Interesting," Krispin commented slowly.

"I do." Tiffany sounded smug. "What about you, Wash? Do you know about vampires? Are you his donor of the month?"

Letting out a slow breath, Wash decided to answer honestly. "Yes. Yes. And No."

Tiffany narrowed her eyes and glanced between them. "What do you mean, no?"

"Just as it sounds, Tiffany," Krispin stated, cocking his head. "Wash is not a donor. He's my partner, soon to be my husband." Upon hearing Tiffany's sneer, Krispin added, "He's permanent."

"No. Not acceptable," Tiffany snapped. "I will not have one of the most powerful men in my city flaunt such deviant behavior."

"Oh, good grief," Carmine grumbled from where she leaned against the desk, her arms crossed over her breasts. "Seriously? What century are you livin' in, lady?"

Tiffany pointed at Carmine. "Shut it, peon."

Carmine allowed her eyes to glow red as she scowled at Tiffany. "Little more than a peon, lady. You say you know about vampires, well you're right in the middle of a bunch of them." She curved her lips in a feral grin, showing off her fangs. "Might wanna show a little respect."

While a hint of fear slipped into Tiffany's scent, she straightened in her seat. "You can't do anything to me."

"We could wipe your mind," Krispin offered, a slight smirk curving his lips. "Make you forget all about us . . . and maybe you'll have a nervous breakdown and quit being the mayor." He exchanged a look with Carmine. "Who should we advocate to take over her position?"

"Just try it," Tiffany snarled, jutting her chin out. "I'm immune."

"Really?" Krispin's eyes hazed, and he stared hard at Tiffany for several heartbeats. Then his irises returned to their cool blue color. "So you are. Still doesn't mean you're safe. Threatening a vampire isn't *safe*."

Tiffany's smile appeared triumphant. "I haven't threatened you . . . yet."

"What do you want?" Wash decided just to throw it out there.

Fortunately, Tiffany answered. "I want you to disappear. I don't care where you go. Just be gone and never return," she stated coldly. Then Tiffany focused on Krispin. "You will marry me and share the gift of your longevity with me. You'll turn me into a vampire, and I'll rule over the city at your side forever."

"Oh, gods." Carmine rolled her eyes as she jerked her thumb in Tiffany's direction. "Delusions of grandeur, table for one."

Unable to help himself, Wash snorted.

Carmine grinned and winked at him.

"And if I don't comply?" Krispin asked, his tone icy.

Tiffany picked up her purse and rummaged inside it. Then she placed a flash drive on Krispin's desk. "Go ahead. Look at it."

With an annoyed sigh, Krispin flicked his finger at it.

Carmine picked it up and inserted it into the side of the TV. The screen flared to life. She used some device in her hand to move a small arrow around the screen. Clicking on an icon, she opened a folder. Inside, were rows upon rows of pictures.

She clicked the first one . . . and groaned. "Bastard."

Wash was going to assume that wasn't the guy's name. The picture showed a red-eyed male with his fangs sunk into the flesh of a woman's neck who wore clubbing clothes. He had her pressed against the rough bricks of a building. While it appeared to be dark in the photo, whatever powerful camera that was used easily picked up the fact that the guy was drinking her blood.

Carmine clicked to the next one . . . and the next . . . and the next, picking up speed. All of the stills contained a similar image. The variations included several different males, whether they were drinking from a male or female, and the locations.

"Well, I guess I'm going to have to speak to the three amigos," Krispin muttered drolly. "And I ask again. What if I don't comply?"

"I'll send those pictures to the cult known as Priests, and this area will be flooded with demon hunters." Tiffany was smiling widely as she waved her hand. "I know, I know. You're not demons, but that's their belief, and I'm happy to use it to get my way."

"First, there's an issue with your request." Krispin's brows furrowed as he shook his head. "Several, actually, but we'll start with the basic one. Vampires are born, not turned. I couldn't make you into a vampire, even if I wanted to, which I never would."

Tiffany's eyes narrowed. "I know that some of the people here who didn't start out as vampires have lived far longer than they should have and haven't aged a day. I've been compiling this information since I was a teenager." She clutched her purse tightly on her lap, her knuckles turning white as her face flushed. Anger radiated from her. "Don't lie to me. I know they paired up with a vampire, and now they're living the good life. I want that, and you're gonna give it to me."

So, she doesn't know about mates, beloveds, or bonding. Probably for the best.

Wash heard Krispin's voice in his head and responded. *Got any bright ideas other than threatening to kill her. I really don't want Priests coming out of the woodwork when you're about to have our child.*

Agreed. And not really. Let's see what she says. Krispin scowled at Tiffany. "I could just kill you now."

Laughing, Tiffany shook her head and waved at the screen, which was once again dark. "I was just seen on a conference call with you, in your office, right here. If something were to happen to me, this would be the first place the police look." Smirking, she added, "And I have all those pictures backed up on several devices at home. If anything happens to me, copies of them will be forwarded to the chief of police, several message boards, and a couple of Priest accounts." With a triumphant look, Tiffany brushed her dark hair over her shoulder. "You're handsome, and I want you. You're going to be mine, and you're going to give me what I want."

"Here's a second issue," Krispin began slowly, obviously choosing his words. "A vampire does not choose who he can give extended life to. That is —"

"Uh, Master Krispin," Carmine cut in softly. "Are you sure you wanna try explaining this to her? She's not going to believe you."

Krispin hummed. "I'm quite certain you're right, Carmine, but I have to try." Scoffing, he waved between himself and Wash. "I mean, it's not like I would ever be able to get it up for her. I'm bonded."

"What's bonded?" Tiffany jumped on that word. "How do you bond?" She leaned forward. "You're already bonded? To who?" A second later, Tiffany's expression looked like a light-bulb had gone off in her head. She sneered at Wash. "You bonded with *him*? *Why*?"

Shrugging, Krispin stated, "When cupid fires his arrow and gives a paranormal a connection with someone, it is what it is." He chuckled softly, saying, "We fell in love. We bonded."

"So if I kill him, the bond will snap, and you can bond with me." Tiffany pulled a gun from her purse.

"Shit!" Wash cried, tired of the entire conversation. He lunged forward, altering his form on instinct. If she did manage to shoot him, at least his thick hide would minimize the damage.

Tiffany screamed as Wash grabbed her wrist. "Demon!"

Even as Wash twisted her arm, Tiffany fired. The report of the blast made his ears ring, which actually hurt worse than the burn to his left side. That didn't stop him from yanking the woman up, twisting her arm, and forcing her to drop the gun.

Screaming and bucking in Wash's hold, Tiffany tried to wrench away. Wash ignored her struggles and scowled at Krispin. He forced her back against his chest and clamped his other hand over her mouth.

"Now what?" Wash growled, his fear for his mate and un-born hatchling causing his voice to come out gruff. "She threatened our bond, and she knows about paranormals. That means she's bound by *our* laws."

Krispin began removing his fake casts. "But she didn't know that offense was punishable by death." Then his nostrils flared. "Are you hit?"

Wash shrugged one shoulder. "Just a scratch."

Growling low in his throat, Krispin stalked around his desk. He walked around him and touched his upper left side. "Blood is seeping from here. Ward." He frowned at Wash.

"You're injured again within my territory. You and I are going to have to talk about this."

Smirking, Wash leaned over and pecked a kiss to Krispin's lips. "I'll let ya spank my ass later, mate."

Krispin groaned, his eyes dilating. Then he huffed a sigh and pointed at Carmine. "Will you take Tiffany and secure her. I'm going to call my men and ask for advice," he admitted, scratching the back of his neck. "What a clusterfuck."

After Carmine had taken Tiffany off Wash's hands, she quickly tied the mayor's hands and used Krispin's tie as a gag. Tiffany's eyes were wide as she stared at Krispin's midsection in horror.

Shiiiit. You shouldn't have gotten up, Krispin. Wash snapped the words into his vampire's mind, staring meaningfully between his bulging midsection and Tiffany.

Sorry, my love. Needed to move, to check on you.

Wash lifted his left arm with a hiss, obeying Ward's orders as the doctor tore apart his shirt to inspect the wound. Ignoring the man's poking and prodding, he racked his brain for a solution. They needed Tiffany's mind gone, but she was part of the one percent of the human population that was immune to a vampire's mind manipulation abilities.

So how . . .

Jerking his focus to Krispin, who was on the phone with Ridger, judging by the voice he heard on the other end of the line, Wash blurted out, "Do you know any demons, or have contact with someone who might?"

Chapter Eleven

U pon hearing Wash's question, Krispin snapped his attention to his beloved. "Ridger, hold on a sec," he ordered, cutting into his second's angry rant. He narrowed his eyes. "A demon?"

Wash nodded, moving toward him even as Ward tried to affix a bandage to his side. "Yeah. A demon is from another plane. They have different magick."

Wrapping his arm around Krispin's waist, Wash stilled, which allowed the clearly annoyed vampire doctor to finish his task. Wash wasn't paying the doc any attention. Instead, he was totally focused on Krispin.

"A demon doesn't look like a human, ever, so they have to use a glamour to appear human when they come to this plane and do their job," Wash pointed out. "That means their magick works on *every* human. No exceptions."

Krispin rubbed his left hand up and down Wash's spine, the move calming him a little. When he hadn't been able to enter Tiffany's mind, he'd hated the spike of trepidation that had risen in him. He had never encountered a human like her before, even though he'd known they existed.

"A demon." Krispin nodded. The idea was sound. Then he frowned and stated into the phone, "Ridger, you and Basques get back here ASAP."

"Already on the move. We'll be there in ten."

Disconnecting the call, Krispin rubbed his right hand over the slightly painful pressure in his back caused by their growing egg. Standard painkillers didn't work for paranormals.

Their higher metabolisms burned through it too swiftly — same reason he could enjoy alcohol while carrying. Fortunately, there was a little help for it.

"Doc, do you have any of that broth Wendy gave us the recipe for?" Krispin asked. Just asking the question meant he was admitting discomfort, but he didn't care. The stuff tasted bad, but it eased his body.

"I'll bring it to you shortly," Ward assured, then hustled from the room.

Blowing out a breath, Krispin glared at the bound and gagged mayor. Then he grabbed his office chair and eased into it. It cradled his body so much more nicely than the wheelchair.

As Krispin booted up his computer, he noticed Wash bringing a chair around to join him behind his desk. He felt the same way. After their little bit of excitement and danger, he needed to be close to his beloved, too.

"What's this?" Wash asked softly, indicating the file Krispin pulled up.

"This is a list of registered covens, the names of their inner circle, and who they're bonded to. Or if they're not bonded." Upon hearing Wash's whistle, Krispin smiled at him. "It's courtesy of the Vampire Council. They keep it on the dark web."

Wash chuckled. "I don't really know what that means."

"I'll teach you all about this later," Krispin promised. "It also lists the same information on members." He pointed. "See, here we are, and there's our names."

"So what are we looking for?"

Krispin typed into the search box the word *demon* and *horseman*. "We're trying to find out if any covens are associated with demons. If they are, well" — he grimaced — "we'll have to decide who we're willing to be indebted to."

"Ah, no one does something for nothing, huh?"

"Afraid that's exactly right," Krispin confirmed with a sigh.

Just as the results of the search pinged on the computer, the office door slammed open. Wash tensed and began to rise, then settled back into his chair. Ridger and Basques stormed into the room. Their visages sported similar expressions of rage, which they immediately pinned on Tiffany.

Before Carmine could close the door, Ward returned, holding a steaming mug.

Relief filled Krispin as he took the dark beverage. Bad tasting or not, the stuff worked. After a sip, he sighed.

"You feeling okay?" Wash asked worriedly.

"I'll be fine. Not long now, anyway," Krispin replied with a smile that he hoped was reassuring.

"So, what's the plan, Kris?" Ridger asked, his voice deep with his anger. "We gearing up for war?"

"Hope not," Krispin replied before taking another sip. He indicated Wash. "My brilliant beloved had a grand idea." Then he indicated the screen, which he turned so everyone could see it.

"Demons?" Basques sounded confused.

Wash quickly explained as Krispin finished his tea.

Ridger blew out a breath. "So, these covens have demons as members," he mused. Then his eyes widened. "And a horseman. Damn."

Basques heaved a sigh on a groan. "So, essentially, we have to decide which one we want to grovel to first. The Esson coven or the Black Forest coven."

"To avert a war, yes," Krispin replied.

"Go to the source? And it's closer." Wash pointed at the screen. "The Black Forest coven is in Montana, and The Horseman of War is bonded with the coven second."

Ridger straightened, crossing his arms over his chest.

"Could a being made to *instigate* war be convinced to manipulate a human's mind to *stop* it?"

"Only one way to find out," Krispin stated.

After clearing his throat, he picked up his phone and dialed the coven's number. The phone rang and rang. By the fourth one, Krispin figured he would have to leave a message. He wished he knew how much time they had before Tiffany's automatic messages would be sent, but he figured there was no way she would share that information.

Then . . . someone picked up. "Black Hills Angus Ranch. This is Raphael speaking. How can I help you?"

Krispin arched a brow upon hearing the very young-sounding man's greeting. "Hello, Raphael. My name is Krispin Stearling." As he spoke, he typed in Raphael's name, searching to see if he was a part of the coven. Seeing that he was bonded with a vampire named Kase, relief filled him. "I'm master of the Maven coven. I would like to speak with Master Dante. Is he available?"

For several heartbeats, the only noise coming through the line was Raphael's breathing. Finally, he squeaked, "R-Really?"

"Yes, *really*, Raphael." Krispin couldn't help but smile in amusement, even under the dire circumstances. "It is of some importance." After a second of hesitation, he added, "Will you tell him it involves the Priests?"

"Oh, shit! The *Priests*? Yeah, yeah. Hold on." Then Krispin heard a clattering noise and figured the young human had dropped the phone onto the desk.

Krispin glanced around at the others, probably thinking the same thing. Evidently, this coven must have had dealings with the Priests recently for Raphael to be all worked up about them. That boded well for their request to be granted.

He waited patiently . . . and waited some more. After around fifteen minutes, he wondered if it would be best to call again. If he tried every thirty minutes, would that be deemed rude?

Or desperate.

Gods, to save my child from facing danger, I —

"This is Dante. Please confirm who you are."

Thank the gods.

"This is Master Krispin Stearling of the Maven coven. Thank you for taking my call, Master Dante."

"Raphael said it was about Priests, so . . . pretty important. Are you facing off against them right now?"

Blunt and to the point. Krispin appreciated that. "Not yet, but the threat is there. It can be prevented, but to do it is . . . complicated."

"When is keeping our people safe *not* complicated?" Dante replied, his tone warming with mirth. "Please know, Master Krispin, I take the threat of Priests very seriously regardless of which coven is facing them. If I can help, I will."

Krispin sighed, relief filling him. "Thank you. So, here's what I'm facing."

Deciding to reward Master Dante's frankness with his own, Krispin told him everything about his situation with Tiffany. As he spoke, he glanced the woman's way. Her face remained flushed, and she continued to glare at them.

"Ah, fuck," Master Dante grumbled when Krispin finally finished. "That's a tough spot to be in."

"Indeed," Krispin confirmed.

"As much as I would *love* to order one of the demons bonded with my people to zip along a lei line and pop into your area, I can't."

Krispin grimaced but held his tongue, since Dante kept speaking.

"They may defer to me in my territory to keep coven hierarchy intact, but they answer to The Horseman of War," Dante told him. "What I can do, however, is contact War on your behalf. If there *is* a conflict brewing in your area, he'll know about it. In that case, I'll send people to help defend you."

That's nice of him.

Krispin smiled upon hearing Wash's words in his mind and nodded at his beloved.

"If there isn't supposed to be a conflict in your area, War will know how to put a stop to the issue."

"Thank you, Master Dante. Either way, I'll be in your debt." Krispin shifted uncomfortably as he tapped his desk. "If there's ever a time when you need assistance, or if there's something you wish in repayment—"

Master Dante's warm chuckle came through the line. "I understand perfectly," he stated. "A boon for the future. One never knows."

"Of course." As much as Krispin hated not having exact parameters set, the other master was doing him a massive favor, so it was his call. "May I know a timeframe of when you'll have this information?"

"Actually, probably pretty quickly," Master Dante revealed. "My second, Monte, just walked in. Hold on."

Even though the other vampire wouldn't be able to see him, he still nodded on reflex. He also heard their conversation faintly through the line.

"Monte, can you ask War if there's supposed to be a conflict with the Priests brewing in Green Springs, Wyoming in the near future?"

"Sure."

Then there was silence . . . but it didn't last long.

A deep voice suddenly sounded in the background. "Chosen mine, why are you asking about Green Springs, Wyoming?"

Krispin decided that had to be War.

It was Master Dante who explained the situation.

While Krispin felt his patience thinning, he held his tongue in check. He would gain nothing by pushing.

"Uh, no," War replied, his deep voice rumbling with displeasure. "The Moirai have given me no indication of any skirmishes to happen anywhere near that area for at least a year. I'm going to send Belial to check this woman's mind. I assume you'll want Gabriel to go with him?"

"That would be fantastic," Dante replied. Then into the phone, he asked, "If that is okay with you, Master Krispin?"

"Of course," Krispin replied. "Your people would be welcome. Should I prepare a suite? Or won't they be staying long?"

"I'm certain they would enjoy a suite, especially if Belial gleans any information about a Priest sect in your area," Master Dante told him. "Gabriel will enjoy running them down and putting a stop to their shenanigans."

Krispin let out a relieved sigh. "Thank you. When should I expect them?"

"They travel along lei lines, and War has already disappeared to track Belial down," Master Dante explained. "It'll probably be pretty quick."

The faster, the better, in Krispin's opinion. He glanced at Ridger and mouthed, "Room." Ridger spun and headed out. Into the phone, Krispin offered, "Thank you again. I'll contact the front desk, so they'll be shown in as soon as they arrive." He gave a pointed look at Basques, who quickly pulled out his phone and stepped away.

"In that case, my best. Thank you for reaching out to me," Master Dante told him. "I'm *always* happy to help deal with Priests."

Then the line went dead.

Krispin blew out a breath and grinned at Wash. "You are brilliant." Then he grabbed his beloved's face and pulled him in for a much-needed kiss.

Ignoring everything—especially the throaty screeches from the trussed-up Tiffany—Krispin delved into Wash's mouth. He teased his tongue over his longer appendage and mapped his mouth anew. Tilting his head a little, he deepened the kiss, sliding to the edge of his seat and pressing closer to his beloved.

It wasn't until some low chuckles filled the room that Krispin pulled himself away from Wash. By then, his erection throbbed against the fly of his suit slacks, and his blood thrummed hotly through his veins. He wanted to crawl onto his gargoyle's lap and rut to completion.

Too bad that will have to wait.

"Later," Wash promised, pecking his lips, then helping Krispin ease back onto his chair.

Once Krispin had his balance — sometimes the unexpected weight of their egg caused him to stumble — he turned his attention to the new arrivals. To his abject pleasure, the scent of Tiffany's fear permeated the room. Rising, he inhaled deeply.

Perhaps it made him a bit perverse, but the bitch had shot his lover, threatened their bond, and had been ready to sic the Priests on him.

A huge black-skinned male stood before him, towering at about six-foot-ten. He sported large, black, bat-like wings, black claws, and black spiraling horns. He wore only a pair of black leather pants and biker boots.

The demon had his arm wrapped around the waist of a muscular, dark-haired vampire. That guy stood about six-foot-even, his eyes were blue in an aristocratic-featured face, and he was already glaring daggers at Tiffany.

Huh. There has to be a story there.

"Welcome, Belial and Gabriel," Krispin stated, dipping his head in acknowledgment of Belial's power. Hell, a bonded demon meant he was over a thousand years old. "I am honored by your assistance."

Gabriel's grin, when he turned it upon him, looked a little feral. His eyes flashed red. "Happy to help locate some more Priests to . . . re-educate."

"Easy, my *amina*," Belial crooned, nuzzling his temple with his lips. "Deep breath. Calm."

Closing his eyes, Gabriel turned his head and inhaled deeply. He was obviously taking in the demon's scent. When he let it out and opened his eyes, they were once again blue.

"Sorry," Gabriel whispered. "Memories."

"I know," Belial replied, squeezing him close against his side. "And we'll keep working hard to make certain that what you went through can never be repeated."

Gabriel's smile, when he tipped his chin up and peered into his beloved's eyes, held a wealth of sadness. "Thank you."

"Anything for you, my *amina*." Belial sealed his mouth over Gabriel's and took him in a deep kiss.

Krispin smiled as he waited for them to come up for air.

It didn't take long.

Belial released Gabriel and turned his attention to Tiffany. "Hello, Tiffany Bickerman." He pulled the coffee table forward and sat before her, turning his back to Krispin. "Let's see what mischief you might be trying to cause."

While Krispin couldn't see what Tiffany saw, he instantly noticed the results. Her eyes glazed, her lips parted, and her face went slack. She even swayed in her seat a bit, but Carmine's hand on her upper arm stilled her.

Carmine, however, pointedly looked to the left, away from the demon's face.

After almost five minutes, Belial turned his head and peered over his shoulder at Krispin. "She could really make a mess," he said on a growl. "What do you want her to do?"

"Yes, I figured as much." Krispin wrapped his arm around Wash. "I would like confirmation that she has destroyed all copies of the photos she took and her mind wiped of anything paranormal."

"And for her to resign as mayor," Ridger piped up, scowling.

Krispin smirked. "Yeah. That, too. I don't care why." Then he frowned. "And make certain she hasn't told anyone else about us."

Gabriel raised his hand. "I want to know how she located the Priests and any information on their organization she might have."

After offering everyone a toothy grin, Belial nodded and returned his focus to Tiffany.

CHAPTER TWELVE

"What do you think Master Dante will want in return?" Basques asked as he swirled the whiskey in his tumbler. "And when?"

Krispin shrugged.

Wash sat with his mate and his friends, along with Basques's beloved, relaxing in his vampire's study. They had drinks in hand, doing their best to relax after the last couple of days' tension.

"Whatever it is, it will have been worth it," Krispin claimed. "The demon forced Tiffany to remove all trace of the pictures and wiped her mind, just as asked."

Ridger laughed. "Even made her resign. That created quite a stir yesterday."

Chuckling, Krispin nodded. He squeezed Wash's hand, clearly pleased they would no longer have to deal with her bullshit.

Wash felt the same and grinned back at him.

"So what was up with Gabriel? He seems a little . . ." Basques's voice trailed off.

"Bloodthirsty?" Ridger offered.

Basques chuckled. "I was going to say intense, but that probably works, too."

"If I had to guess, personal experience with the Priests, and not in a good way," Krispin mused. "You remember years ago we had the Council Enforcer come through with warnings of how the Priests were capturing and torturing our kind?" When Ridger and Basques nodded, he tipped his drink in the general direction of the quarters the pair had been given. "My guess is he was one of them."

"Damn," Basques muttered as Ridger let out a low whistle.

"Just a guess," Krispin repeated. "I—" He paused, hissing.

Wash noticed the tension thrumming through Krispin's body and eased from his chair. Dropping to his knees before his mate, he rubbed his thighs. He spotted the ripple in his vampire's abdomen.

When Wash lifted his gaze and met Krispin's gaze, his mate dipped his chin in a slow nod.

"It's begun," Wash stated, rising. He took Krispin's tumbler and set both his and his mate's aside. Turning, he focused on the trio, who had also risen. "I need one of you to fetch Ward. I'm taking him to our suite."

"You're not going to the hospital wing?" Ridger questioned, clearly concerned.

Wash shook his head. "No. We discussed it. Krispin wants to birth in our room."

"We'll help you," Basques stated, stepping forward with Dloben.

"Meet you there," Ridger hustled from the room.

Sliding his arms under Krispin's upper back and knees, Wash eased him into his arms. "If you could open doors and clear hallways, I'd appreciate it," he told the pair. "I'm sure Krispin would like as few of his people to see him like this as possible."

"Yup." Basques opened the door wide, which Ridger had left half open in his haste. "To the left. Shorter distance on the floor's loop."

Wash appreciated the reminder. He also made a mental note to start exploring his surroundings more. This was his home now, so he should be familiar with it.

Basques eased Wash's keycard out of his back pocket, and he was suddenly reminded of the vampire doing the same thing the first day he'd arrived. He'd been jealous then, of the man touching Krispin so intimately. So much had changed since that day.

Dloben ran ahead, confirming the hallways were clear. At one point, he engaged in conversation with someone, allowing Wash to turn the corner without them seeing anyone. Once they arrived at the suite he shared with Krispin, Wash watched Basques open the door.

The vampire did the same for the bedroom door, too. Then he hustled to the bed and yanked off the comforter and top sheet. Dloben had already arrived, and he carried a stack of towels. Those he spread out on the mattress.

Finally, Wash was able to ease his sweating, trembling mate onto the mattress.

"Wash? Krispin?" Ward's voice sounded through the hall.

"In here," Wash replied. "But I need everyone to leave until it's time for him to push."

"Wait, here." Hustling into the room, Ward held out a small, clear packet. "Have him take these."

Wash saw two tablets inside. "What is it?"

"Paranormal pain medicine," Ward told him. "I reached out to the paranormal medical community, and it turns out a shifter pack in Colorado has a few scientists that created them."

Narrowing his eyes, Wash had to ask, "Are they safe?"

"Perfectly," Ward assured. "Start with just one. Now that the egg is no longer attached to him and beginning to move inside his body, it's just fine."

Knowing he had to take the doc at his word, he nodded.

Dloben appeared with a couple of bottles of water as well as a pile of cloths—some damp, some dry. He placed them on the nightstand.

"Thanks." Wash pointed toward the door. "Everyone, please stay in the front room unless I call for you."

"I should really be here to monitor his progress," Ward countered, glancing from Wash to the bed and back again.

"No," Krispin ordered. "Do as my beloved wishes."

"If I need you, I'll call," Wash assured.

Even though they appeared uncertain, the group left, closing the door behind them.

Wash turned and focused on Krispin, taking in his shallow breaths and shuddering body. "Four to eight hours of this," he grumbled as he dropped the bottles on the nightstand. He opened up the pills and pulled one out. "I'm so sorry, my mate."

"Stop apologizing," Krispin countered, taking the pill. "We've done enough of that." After allowing Wash to help him drink some water, he added, "Besides, we're about to have a son. This is a time for celebration."

"Gods, I love you," Wash whispered, reveling in the way his mate looked at things.

Krispin's brows shot up. Then he grinned widely. "Love you, too, beloved."

Realizing what he'd said, and what his mate had said back, happiness flooded him.

Until Krispin's brows furrowed in pain.

Wash grabbed one of the damp cloths and laid it over Krispin's sweating brow. Then he made quick work of removing his vampire's clothes. Due to not wanting to move the man, he mostly shredded them with his claws.

Krispin chuckled roughly. "Effective."

"I thought so," Wash murmured with a wink. "Now, for a pain remedy that doesn't involve chemicals."

"Oh?"

"Mmm-hmmm," Wash confirmed.

Wash grabbed the lube from the drawer and climbed onto the bed. Easing between Krispin's calves, he carefully helped his mate spread his legs wide. Then he poured a healthy dollop of slick onto his fingers.

"You remember what Wendy said about stretching?"

Krispin groaned. "Oh, gods. Don't remind me."

"It was good advice," Wash countered.

Then Wash dipped his head and began nuzzling Krispin's ball sack. He licked at the soft, sensitive flesh while lowering his fingers to rub beneath it. At the same time, he reached up and teased at Krispin's nipples.

"Oh, gods, Wash," Krispin muttered. "I-I'm not s-sure this is the right time."

"It's the perfect time," Wash countered, moving his lubed fingers to Krispin's hole. "Nature's pain remedy."

Sticking out his long tongue, Wash wrapped it around Krispin's soft penis. He gently slid his way up the length, tugging lightly. By the time he reached the vampire's crown, he felt the flesh begin to harden.

Perfect.

While working on Krispin's dick, Wash eased a finger inside his chute. He wiggled it around, massaging his inner muscles. Lubing and stretching the channel, he stimulated his lover.

To Wash's pleasure, Krispin's hisses slowly transformed into soft moans and sighs. His cock thickened nearly to full mast, and he reached down and threaded his fingers through Wash's hair. Looking up his vampire's body, he saw the gleam of relaxation enter his deep-blue eyes.

Wash figured it was a mix of whatever was in the pill, but he knew his ministrations helped, too. Easing in a second finger, he sucked on Krispin's flared head. He wasn't in any hurry to get his mate off. He just wanted to offer stimulation.

Krispin must have realized that, for he slowly began relaxing his body. His knees turned out, offering more space between his thighs. He rubbed at Wash's scalp, murmuring his thanks.

Making certain to keep any pressure off of Krispin's abdomen, Wash continued to mouth and suckle his length and crown. He applied more lube before returning his dry hand to his mate's nipples. Then he eased a third finger into Krispin's channel, nudging at his prostate ever-so-gently.

Wash didn't know how long he continued his ministrations. His jaw began to tire, and his thighs and abdominals burned from the strain of balancing. While his cock ached behind his loincloth, he didn't fear getting off, since his actions were devoted to relaxing his mate. He did his best to ignore it all. His only goal was to distract Krispin's body from the pain.

When Krispin's erection began to drip pre-cum into his mouth, Wash smiled. He lapped it up, enjoying his vampire's unique flavor. His mate's erection immediately offered him more.

"Gods, but this feels good, my beloved," Krispin muttered. He hummed, then shifted his hips a little. "But, um —"

Wash peered up Krispin's body and noticed his furrowed brows. Popping off his mate's prick, he whispered, "What is it? Anything for you."

To Wash's surprise, he saw a flush sweep up Krispin's neck for a new reason. "I think I need to push."

Understanding flooded Wash, and he nodded. "Two seconds. I'm gonna get you off, give you that little extra bit of pleasure," he promised. "Then I'll get the doc, and we'll push."

Krispin nodded, his panting taking on a slightly different sound.

Wash grabbed the lube and poured more onto his fingers. As he swallowed Krispin's cock to the root, he moved his dry hand to his vampire's balls, knowing how sensitive they were and how much he enjoyed them being played with. Then he eased a fourth finger into Krispin's channel, stretching him wide.

Starting a swift bobbing with his mouth, Wash sucked and worked Krispin's length in his most favorite ways. He teased at his frenulum, swept his tongue over his head, and dipped the tip of his appendage into his slit. Then he took him deep and swallowed around him.

All the while, Wash massaged Krispin's prostate and rolled his balls.

"Uuuuhhhhh, Wash!" Krispin cried.

Then Wash's mouth was filled with burst after burst of seed. He swallowed and swallowed some more. As much as he wanted to continue playing—to coax as much out of Krispin as possible—he knew something else took precedence.

Popping off Krispin's still hard dick, Wash eased his fingers free as it pulsed one more burst of cream. He grabbed a dry towel and draped it over his vampire's groin. "Doc!" Wash hollered, knowing the vampire would easily be able to hear him.

Grabbing a damp towel, Krispin began wiping off his hands. Then he wiped as his face. He'd just replaced the damp cloth on Krispin's forehead when Ward hustled into the room.

"How's he doing?" the vampire asked, sweeping his gaze over him. "Appears a bit flushed, but how's your pain level, Master?"

"Not too bad," Krispin replied, although some tension was definitely leeching back into his tone. "Think I'm ready to push."

"On the shorter end of things, then," Ward commented. "Good. It's only been four and a half hours."

That explains why my jaw is sore.

"I'm going to slide my hands under the towel to check the egg's location. Try not to freak out on me."

Upon hearing the doc's words, Wash met his gaze and nodded but kept his mouth shut. Instead, he threaded the fingers of one hand into Krispin's hair, scraping his scalp gently. He took his mate's fingers in the other, giving him something to hold onto.

"Yes, yes," Ward said, bobbing his head. "You're definitely there. Good. Good."

Does the doc sound nervous to you? Wash couldn't help but mentally ask his vampire for his opinion.

"Okay, push," Ward ordered.

Ga! Don't distract me!

Krispin's fingers clamped onto Wash's as he obeyed the order.

"That's the way, my love," Wash encouraged, doing his best not to wince at Krispin's tight grip. "You're on the homestretch. Almost there."

"Stop and take a few breaths," the doctor told him.

Krispin panted harshly, his face contorting with discomfort.

"Push!"

"Ahhhh!" Krispin growled unintelligibly. Then he gasped. "Oh!"

"Congratulations, Master Krispin," Ward cried. "Hand me a damp towel, Wash."

Since Krispin wasn't releasing him, Wash twisted and awkwardly obeyed. He grabbed a dry one, too, and handed it to Ward as soon as he was ready for it. Then the doctor held up their prize—a large, leathery egg covered in a deep burnished golden color.

"Your future son, Master Krispin." Ward held it out.

When Krispin just stared in shock, Wash eased his hand from his mate's. He took the towel-wrapped egg and cradled it to his chest. Leaning over Krispin, he held it close to him.

"Look at what we made together," Wash whispered, in awe of the fact that he held knew life. While he noticed the doc cleaning Krispin up out of the corner of his eye, he did his best to keep his mate's focus on the egg. It wasn't that tough. Krispin couldn't seem to tear his gaze away from it.

Finally, Krispin reached out and skimmed the pads of his

forefingers over the egg's curved edge. "It's so warm," he murmured. "That was inside me."

"Yeah." Wash didn't know what else to say.

Krispin rested his palm on the egg for a few seconds, rubbing over it lightly. Then he met Wash's gaze, his expression serious. "Wash, I love you, but let's make certain the next one is planned. Okay?"

Wash chuckled softly as he nodded. "Most definitely." Leaning down, he pecked a kiss to Krispin's lips.

"Is it safe to come in, yet?" Basques called. "We wanna see!"

Chuckling, Wash called. "Just a minute more." Then he held out the egg, and that time, Krispin quickly took it. Wash turned and found the doc already bundling up all the dirty towels. He'd even managed to pull the soiled ones out from under Krispin. "Can I dress him?"

Ward nodded, beaming at him. "If it's something soft. His yoga pants. Lounging pants or sweats."

Wash nodded and crossed to their dresser. He pulled a pair of soft blue lounging pants out of the second drawer. After a quick glance over his shoulder and seeing the doctor heading toward the door, he yanked off the final towel. Then he helped his mate and master into the lounging pants.

Once Krispin was settled comfortably, the comforter back on the bed and pulled partway up his body, he called for the others to enter. He placed a few pillows behind his vampire, then settled on the bed beside him.

As everyone clustered around the bed and *oohed* and *aahed* about the miracle they'd created, Wash realized how swiftly life could change.

Just over three months, and I have a new home, an amazing dedicated mate, and a new family.

"What are you smiling about?" Krispin murmured, drawing Wash's attention.

Taking in his formidable vampire master's sparkling blue

eyes, Wash grinned. "Just happy."

Krispin reached up and cradled Wash's nape. "Me, too."

With a bit of gentle pressure, Krispin urged Wash to bend close. Only too happy to comply, he took his mate's mouth in a soft meeting of lips that he intended to do over and over again.

For the rest of my days.

You may also enjoy the following from eXtasy Books Inc:

ArMaDillo Packin'
Charlie Richards

Excerpt

"How's she handlin'?"

Ronald Oleander—Ronnie to his friends—smirked as he flicked his gaze to Adam Kingston's broad back where he drove his Harley a few feet in front of him. The white tiger shifter had asked that very question three times so far—twice the previous day and now just then. He knew the man was worried about him, as this was Ronnie's first road trip with him, but come on!

"Just like I told you yesterday," Ronnie replied, doing his best to keep his exasperation out of his voice. "She's handlin' like a dream. After all, you fitted her to my body type."

It was true, too.

Ronnie had met Adam almost eight years before when he'd been thirteen years old. He'd been a scrawny, gangly teen, who'd only learned how to shift into his moose form the prior year. His sister, Heather, had been seventeen. They'd been on the run, and Adam had saved them from wolf shifters.

When his older brother, Noah, had caught up with them,

they'd discovered Adam was his brother's mate. At the time, Adam had been part of a shifter biker gang. The group had taken them in, cared for them, and fixed the mess that had been caused by the son of their herd's alpha.

Of course, there was more to it than that, but the gist was that Adam and his people had saved them.

"Just makin' sure nothin' has changed since then," Adam replied through the speaker in Ronnie's helmet, reminding him to focus on the road.

A drifting mind of a motorcycle rider could be a dangerous thing.

"I know," Ronnie confirmed, smiling as he enjoyed the wind on his face. "If anything feels even slightly off, you know I'll say something."

"Good." Adam turned his head and peered at Noah, who was driving an equally lovely Kingpin next to him. "What about yours, babe?"

Noah looked Adam's way, allowing Ronnie to see his grin. "Perfect as always."

Adam's grunt came through the speaker.

Ronnie sighed happily, relishing the rumble of the Harley Electra Glide Ultra between his thighs. The bike had been bigger than what his brother had expected him to pick for his first motorcycle, but over the last few years, he'd grown like a weed and bulked up. He knew it had everything to do with his moose shifter genetics. At twenty-one years old, Ronnie found himself standing at six-foot-three, and neither Noah nor Adam could say if he had stopped growing, yet.

He'd needed something he could keep even if he added another couple of inches.

"Are you comfortable on these windy roads, Ronnie?" Noah asked, glancing over his shoulder at him. "We're not going too fast, are we?"

Ronnie rolled his eyes even as he grinned. "I'm good, bro. Don't worry. I got this."

"It's just, it's your first time out on a road trip with us,"

Noah continued, expressing his concern. "So if you need to stop and rest, let us know."

"Relax, babe," Adam rumbled, glancing his mate's way. "He's fine. He can handle her."

Ronnie warmed at the praise. "Thanks, Adam."

Noah chuckled. "Naw, babe. Ronnie wouldn't ever be able to handle a her."

Adam's deep laughter sounded even over the roar of the engines. "True dat."

Shaking his head, Ronnie joined in the laughter. They were right, after all. When he'd only been thirteen, he'd been confused about his feelings. While the other boys in their herd had been beginning to notice girls, Ronnie hadn't been.

It all became crystal clear when Adam had introduced him to his alpha—Kontra Belikov. The grizzly shifter had been huge with silver-flecked hair and an imposing bearing. Instead of being afraid of the man, he'd found himself enamored with him. While the gang had been in town, Ronnie had followed Kontra around like a puppy dog.

Looking back on that, Ronnie felt a bit of embarrassment. The bear shifter hadn't minded, even though he'd probably scented his arousal a time or two. Of course, the man wasn't interested in him as more than a mentor. Plus, well, Ronnie had been only thirteen at the time, so even if he hadn't had a mate, no way would Kontra have touched him.

"Oh, hey," Adam exclaimed, glancing over his shoulder at him. "Did you tell that human guy you were hookin' up with that you were goin' out of town?"

Ronnie felt his cheeks heat as Noah barked, "What? What human guy?"

"Uh—" Ronnie could see Adam's back muscles tighten, even under his leather jacket.

"It was nothin'," Ronnie quickly stated, doing his best to smooth it over. "Just a human guy I was studying the motorcycle test with. And, yeah. I told him I was headed out with you all."

With the way they were roaring down the road on motorcycles, Ronnie mentally crossed his fingers that his brother wouldn't be able to scent the little fib.

"Good," Noah grumbled. "The thought of you doing anything with anyone is—" He stopped and shook his head.

Ronnie spotted Adam eyeballing him in his side mirror, so he shrugged.

Adam refocused on the road.

As a young horny shifter, Ronnie wanted to get his rocks off as much as the next man. Unfortunately, after his sister, Heather, had bonded with the alpha of their herd, no one would touch the alpha-mate's younger brother. He'd turned his attention to humans.

Ronnie had always been discreet with his hook-ups. He would find a like-minded guy in the next town over, and they would have a little fun. He made certain he never saw a guy more than a couple of times, since he didn't want to lead anyone on.

Being a shifter, Ronnie knew he had a fated mate out there somewhere. Plus, he was young. No way was he ready to settle down.

One day the prior spring, Ronnie had been running late for his shift at the garage where he worked with Adam. He'd thought the soapy wipe-down would be enough. It hadn't been.

When Ronnie walked into the garage, Adam had just closed the office door where he knew Noah was doing paperwork. The cat shifter had grabbed his arm, stopping his forward momentum. He'd not-so-discreetly sniffed.

Ronnie had felt his face go up in flames.

Fortunately, Adam had chuckled and warned, "Shower next time." He'd patted him on his back as he moved around him. Just when Ronnie had thought that would be it, Adam had turned to face him, walking backward. "And even if it's a guy, make sure to use a condom. Don't want any suspicions, yeah?"

Nodding on instinct, Ronnie had begun to follow him. After all, he needed to get to work.

Adam had spun around, then asked over his shoulder, "You need me to pick up rubbers or lube for ya?" Then he paused and pivoted, staring at him with his eyebrows furrowed. "I guess I just assumed." Rubbing the back of his neck, Adam lowered his voice. "You have had the discussion about safe sex, right? Proper prep and all that?"

Ronnie hadn't thought his face could get any hotter . . . but it had.

"Yeah," Ronnie had muttered. "I'm good."

After a quick nod, Adam had muttered, "Well, you know where I am if you ever need anything." Then the shifter had gotten to work.

They'd never spoken of it again, which was just fine by Ronnie.

The fact that Adam had remembered that he might be leaving someone behind was sort of . . . nice.

ABOUT THE AUTHOR

Charlie started writing fantasy when she was eight, and after stumbling onto her first erotic romance at age nineteen, she realized her true calling. She now focuses on writing gay erotic romance, normally of the paranormal variety, with heroes of all kinds. With the help and support of her husband, Charlie finally fulfilled one of her life-long goals . . . move to acreage with her horses. You can often find her curled up with her laptop and a cup of tea or glass of wine, creating her next adventure. Charlie enjoys exploring the mountains of her new Oregon home on horseback, 4-wheeler, or motorcycle.

She can be reached at ch.richards2010@yahoo.com
Or visit her at www.charlie-richards.com

www.ingramcontent.com/pod-product-compliance
Lightning Source LLC
Chambersburg PA
CBHW060638130626
46555CB00002B/866